Emily Windsnap

and the
Pirate Prince

D0950224

Novels by Liz Kessler

The Tail of Emily Windsnap
Emily Windsnap and the Monster from the Deep
Emily Windsnap and the Castle in the Mist
Emily Windsnap and the Siren's Secret
Emily Windsnap and the Land of the Midnight Sun
Emily Windsnap and the Ship of Lost Souls
Emily Windsnap and the Falls of Forgotten Island
Emily Windsnap and the Pirate Prince
Emily Windsnap and the Tides of Time

Philippa Fisher and the Fairy Godsister
Philippa Fisher and the Dream-Maker's Daughter
Philippa Fisher and the Fairy's Promise

A Year Without Autumn

North of Nowhere

Has Anyone Seen Jessica Jenkins?

Kessler, Liz, author.
Emily Windsnap and the pirate
prince
2019
3330522 79   8
gi   0   8/2

Emily Windsnap

and the

Pirate Prince

LIZ KESSLER

illustrations by ERIN FARLEY

CANDLEWICK PRESS

This is a work of fiction. Names, characters, places, and incidents are either products of the author's imagination or, if real, are used fictitiously.

Text copyright © 2019 by Liz Kessler
Illustrations copyright © 2019 by Erin Farley

All rights reserved. No part of this book may be reproduced, transmitted, or stored in an information retrieval system in any form or by any means, graphic, electronic, or mechanical, including photocopying, taping, and recording, without prior written permission from the publisher.

First published in Great Britain by Orion Children's Books, a division of the Orion Publishing Group

First U.S. trade paperback edition 2020

Library of Congress Catalog Card Number 2018961117
ISBN 978-1-5362-0299-1 (hardcover)
ISBN 978-1-5362-1312-6 (trade paperback)

19 20 21 22 23 24 LSC 10 9 8 7 6 5 4 3 2 1

Printed in Crawfordsville, IN, U.S.A.

This book was typeset in Bembo.

Candlewick Press
99 Dover Street
Somerville, Massachusetts 02144

visit us at www.candlewick.com

This book is dedicated to Tracy Miracle,
in thanks for a decade of working with someone who
truly lives up to her name, and also for that moment,
mid–book tour, when you said, "Have you done pirates yet?
How about a pirate prince?"

It is also dedicated to Jakob, Michelle, Anaïs, Tom, Hessel, and
Maarten, and my crewmates aboard the beautiful Morgenster
in February 2017. A wonderful and very inspiring trip.
And don't worry, none of the characters are based on you,
even if I borowed a few of your names.

Ordinary riches can be stolen from a man.
Real riches cannot. In the treasury-house
of your soul, there are infinitely precious
things, that may not be taken from you.

—Oscar Wilde

Chapter One

Question. You're offered a choice: cross the ocean in a magical golden chariot accompanied by dolphins and whales with your dad and your best friend, or take a luxury five-star cruise with your mom and your boyfriend. Which do you go for?

To be fair, I suppose that most people don't get offered these options.

But I'm not most people. And this actually *was* a decision I had to make.

We'd all been on vacation together. It was supposed to be a relaxing week in the sun. It turned out to involve a near-death experience in the world's biggest waterfall, a brush with a five-hundred-year-old giant, and an earthquake that nearly caused a world-threatening tsunami.

Just your average week.

Just *my* average week anyway! It certainly seemed like it lately.

The one good thing to come out of it was that we'd managed to help prevent a catastrophe from destroying the nearby islands. As a mark of gratitude, the people from the resort where we'd been staying had booked us cabins on a luxury cruise to take us home. As well as all the usual stuff that grown-ups love, like ballrooms and chandeliers and all that, the ship had a whole deck for kids, with its own theme park! We'd heard there were waterslides, climbing walls, about a hundred different clubs, and all-you-can-eat buffets.

Neptune was grateful too. We'd stopped a tsunami that could have threatened entire continents. Not that it was his fault, but he probably would have gotten the blame. Even Neptune doesn't want something like that on his conscience. And since he never likes to be outdone, he matched the luxury cruise by offering his best chariot, his finest dolphins, and even a whale to escort us home.

Which was why I had the dilemma.

My best friend, Shona, is a mermaid. So am I, but only when I go in water. Shona's a mermaid all the time, so she took Neptune up on his offer. His chariot can ride on the water, but it mostly dives down and powers through the sea. My dad is a merman, so he'd be going with Shona.

Mom and her best friend, Millie, were already getting excited about the luxury cruise. Well, Millie was. Mom was half excited and half sad.

"I just wish your dad and I could share one of these wonderful things with each other," she said to me as we walked along the soft golden beach one last time. Mom's human, so she didn't have the magical chariot option. "It's never as much fun on your own."

"You won't be on your own, Mom," I reassured her.

She took my hand as we walked. "I know. Millie will be there, but it's not the same." She sighed heavily, and I knew what I had to do.

"Mom, would you feel better about it if I was there too?"

Mom squeezed my hand. "Really?" she asked, her eyes sparkling with hope. "You'd do that for me?"

"Of course I would, Mom. I don't want you feeling sad."

She pulled me into a hug. "Oh, thank you, darling. I feel better about it already. We'll have a nice time together."

I laughed as Mom squeezed me so hard I could hardly breathe. "We will," I agreed, once she'd let me go.

And I meant it. For one thing, the ship *did* sound amazing. And for another, Aaron had already told me he was choosing the cruise over the chariot.

Aaron's my boyfriend, and he's a semi-mer like I am. He'd had an even more life-changing week than the rest of us. Turned out the giant was a distant relative of his, and Aaron had promised to come back to live at Forgotten Island with his mom.

Which meant that this would be one of the last chances we'd get to spend time together.

Aaron had chosen the ship as soon as he'd heard about the theme park. He'd grown up without anything like that in his life. The closest thing he'd seen to one was the fairground at the end of Brightport pier. This one sounded about ten times better than that—and it was on a ship!

"A luxury cruise," Mom murmured as she kicked at the soft sand. "Sounds good, doesn't it?"

"Yeah," I said. I had to admit, it did.

"You're sure you've got everything?" Mom asked Dad as he and Shona swam alongside the jetty to see us off. We were heading to a small boat that was going to take us out to the ship. The hotel people had already sent our luggage ahead of us. Millie was pacing ahead while Aaron and I walked beside Mom. Dad and Shona were staying for another day before Neptune's chariot arrived for them.

Dad laughed. "What do we need, exactly?" he asked. "We've got ourselves; Neptune and his team are on their way. We're all set!"

Mom stopped walking. "Just—be careful. Look after yourself, and look after Shona," she said. Her voice wobbled as she spoke.

Dad stretched his arms out of the water. One of his hands was closed around something. "Come here," he said.

"I can't—I'll get my dress wet."

"Who cares?" Dad laughed. "Come on. I've got a present for you."

"A present? What for?"

Dad shrugged. "Because I love you," he said simply. "And so you will know I'm always with you, even when I'm not."

Mom pulled off her shoes and crouched down on the jetty. She hitched her dress above her knees and dangled her legs over the side.

Aaron and I sat on the edge of the jetty with her as Shona swam up to join us. The three of us watched as Dad opened his hand. He held his palm out to Mom; I leaned over to look at it.

He was holding out a fine gold chain. It had a pendant on it: two interlocked hearts — one made of tiny diamonds, the other of gold. A mermaid's tail was looped around the hearts. The diamonds glinted in the sunlight.

Mom clapped a hand over her mouth. "Jake," she whispered. "It's beautiful."

"Like you," he replied.

The three of us stared. Mom was right. The necklace was the most delicate, sparkling thing I'd ever seen.

"Mr. Windsnap, that necklace is swishy!" Shona breathed.

Dad grinned. "I know!"

"Where on earth did you get it?" Mom asked.

"From Neptune!"

"Neptune?" I burst out. Neptune was the king of all the seas, and Dad's boss. He wasn't known for his generosity or for giving out gifts for no reason. "Why did Neptune give you a necklace?"

"He told me he'd been planning to give me something anyway, in recognition of my hard work since I joined his team. And then everything happened last week and he said he wanted to show his gratitude to our family in a manner that was fitting for the occasion."

I could just imagine Neptune saying something like that. "It's gorgeous," I said.

"Apparently, it's a rare item from one of his most treasured collections," Dad added proudly.

Mom was still staring. "Come here," Dad said. "Let me put it on you."

Mom tipped her head forward and Dad swished his tail so he could reach up to fasten it around her neck.

Mom threw her arms around Dad. "I love it," she said. "And I love you."

I made a face at Aaron and Shona.

Aaron stood up and brushed his legs off. "Come on, then," he said.

I looked at Shona in the water. I wasn't quite ready to say good-bye to my best friend. It was only going to be a few days, but after everything we'd been through in the last week, that felt too long.

"Wait." I glanced at Mom and Dad. "I'll meet you at the end of the jetty. I'm going to swim up there with Shona," I said, pulling off my shoes. "OK, Mom?"

Mom was still smooching with Dad. "Just be careful," she said. "And don't be late."

"I won't. I'll be there in five minutes."

I already had my swimsuit on under my clothes, so I wriggled out of my shorts and T-shirt. I perched on the jetty for a moment, feeling the water on my toes.

Then I slid into the water. It was warm and smooth like caramel. I wanted to melt into it.

I closed my eyes as I ducked my head under, letting the water wrap me up.

A moment later, I got the familiar feeling that had become as important to me as breathing or sleeping. My toes began to tingle. Then they went numb. The tingly numbness traveled up my calves and thighs as I felt my legs stiffen and fuse together. A moment later, my legs disappeared; in their place my tail formed.

I was a mermaid.

I flicked my tail and dived down in the water. Shona dived with me, and we swam across the bay.

"Are you sure you're OK with this?" I asked her.

Shona's blond hair swirled around her as she swam. "Travel home to Shiprock courtesy of Neptune's golden chariot and his finest dolphins?" she asked. She flicked her tail to spread a sparkling arc of bubbles all around her. "Hmmm, let me think."

I laughed. "I just don't want you to be lonely or feel left out or anything," I said.

"Honestly, it's totally fine. I promise."

"OK, good. I'll miss you, though," I said as we swam on. The water was so clear that I could see the sandy seabed below us. Fish darted by, scurrying on with their lives as we swam past them.

"I'll miss you too," Shona replied, lazily flicking her tail as she floated along beside me. "But just think how much we'll have to tell each other when we meet up again!"

"That's true," I agreed.

Shona grinned. "Come on. I'll race you to the end of the jetty."

We spun our tails and zoomed through the water.

As I pulled myself out and waited for my legs to return, Mom called over. "Let's get going."

"See you on the other side," I called to Shona and Dad as I rejoined Mom and Aaron.

Shona replied with a wave and then dived down under the water, flicking her tail and leaving a rainbow arc of water behind her.

"See you soon, little 'un," Dad called to me. "Have fun!"

"We will!" I called back.

As I watched Dad and Shona swim away, I felt as if they were taking a piece of me with them.

"Come on!" Millie called. A little speedboat was bobbing in the water below her. "The boat's leaving in two minutes!"

The three of us ran to catch up with Millie and board the boat that would take us to the cruise ship: our home for the next few days.

I linked Mom's arm as the speedboat headed out of the bay. "It won't be long," I said. "Then we'll get back to normal life together."

Mom softly patted my arm. "I can't wait," she admitted.

I leaned my head on Mom's shoulder and looked out to sea as we bounced through the waves.

When we rounded the headland a huge white gleaming ship came into sight. It had seven floors, with balconies all around the sides, and a brightly polished deck in the back. The boat's name, the *Sunbeam,* was written in gold letters on the hull.

Even from this distance, I could see the theme park slides on the top deck. Aaron nudged me and grinned.

I stared as we drew closer to the ship. A door silently opened as we approached the stern, and we drove through the door and into the ship's belly.

"This is your stop," our driver said as he threw a rope to a couple of guys in ship's uniform who'd come down to meet us. The driver kept the boat steady as he helped us off the speedboat. "Have fun!" he said, giving his engine a couple of revs. Then he unhooked his boat and drove off.

The men welcomed us aboard and led the way. "We'll show you to your cabins," one of them said. He smiled as he added, "I think you'll be happy."

As we walked through the ship—up a spiral staircase, across marble floors, past floor-to-ceiling windows, and under enormous chandeliers—Mom and Millie pointed and gasped at the finery. Aaron and I grabbed handfuls of candy from bowls along the way.

Finally, we reached our deck. We had four cabins along the same corridor. And when I say cabins, I actually mean luxury suites.

I walked on the soft carpet into my suite. It was huge. I opened the bathroom door. It had its own whirlpool bath. The walls had pictures of dolphins and whales. The soap dispenser was in the shape of a snow globe, and the toilet paper had crossword puzzles on it!

Going back into the main part of the cabin, I sat on the big double bed. It felt so soft and springy I was tempted to jump up and down on it like I used to when I was a kid. Maybe later.

Dragging myself up, I looked around. There was a sofa and a large-screen television. I checked the list. Fifty children's channels! Not that I was likely to sit around watching TV with everything else to do on this ship.

I walked over to the patio doors that led out to my own balcony. I threw them open and went outside.

"Hi!" Mom was on the adjoining balcony. "Well, what about this?" she asked. "Think we're going to have a nice journey home?"

"Hmmm, let me think," I replied. "Possibly!"

As the ship began to sail out to sea, I couldn't stop grinning. For once, I was pretty sure I could say that *nothing* would ruin this trip.

Chapter Two

*T*his is pretty cool, isn't it?" Aaron said as he passed a plate back to me.

"Uh-huh," I replied.

It was our first evening on board the *Sunbeam* and we were in the ship's ballroom, lining up at the buffet. We'd already had our main courses and had reached the important part: dessert.

My stomach was almost full to bursting, but my brain still wanted more. It was a difficult decision. Chocolate fondue with marshmallows and strawberries, mint chocolate-chip ice cream, or Black Forest cupcakes?

I settled on a small portion of all three as Aaron passed me a spoon.

"Wow," I murmured as I took it from him. "This ship! Even the spoons are fancy." It looked like sterling silver, with an ornate pattern chiseled around the end.

We were making our way back to our table when a crackle came over the loudspeaker. It was followed by a woman clearing her throat.

"Ladies and gentlemen, I hope you are all enjoying your dinner. For those who have just joined us, I'm Greta and I'm the Entertainment Director. Welcome to the *Sunbeam*. I hope you have a wonderful stay with us. And I hope you have your dancing shoes with you for our band tonight."

Aaron nudged me. "What do you think? A bunch of old people doing a soft-shoe shuffle, or worth checking out?" he asked.

I shrugged and grimaced. "Both?"

Greta was still talking. "The band will be here shortly and the music will begin in about twenty minutes. Have a great evening, everyone."

We got back to our table and started in on our desserts.

As promised, the band began setting up on

the stage at the far end of the room, and it wasn't long before they started playing. I didn't recognize the songs but most people were tapping along or nodding their heads.

Millie turned to Mom. "They're good, aren't they?" she said.

"They are," Mom agreed. In a quieter voice, she added, "I just wish I had someone to dance with."

"Do you want to dance with me, Mrs. Windsnap?" Aaron asked as he wiped his mouth and put his spoon down.

Mom laughed. "That's very sweet of you but not exactly what I meant. You two should, though."

Aaron turned to me. "You want to?" he asked.

The song had finished and the singer started talking. "OK, that got the older crowd going. Now let's play a few modern ones for the youngsters."

They started a song I knew: the one where you all do the same movements, kind of impersonating a chicken. We used to do it at school.

"It's the chicken dance!" I said.

"The *what*?" Aaron asked as he let me pull him out of his seat.

"I'll show you. You just basically copy the guy at the front."

Aaron glanced at the band leader, currently bent over and flapping his arms around. People were getting up to join in. A bunch of little kids at the front squealed as they copied his movements.

"OK." Aaron laughed as we made our way onto the dance floor. "But this might not be my finest hour. I'm not very good at following a routine."

We joined in with the dance. Aaron was right. He was terrible at it! He kept flapping his arms when everyone else was bending their legs, and he kept clapping when the rest of us were twirling around in circles.

I was clutching my stomach by the time the song finished. "I'm in pain from laughing so much," I said.

"I'm in pain from banging into people!" Aaron laughed as he followed me back across the dance floor.

Mom was approaching the table with a tray of drinks. "Coke for you two, OK?" she asked as she handed us each a glass. "Mojitos with an extra twist of lime for Millie and me."

We clinked glasses. "Cheers," I said.

"To a wonderful trip home," Mom added.

I was standing by the table and looking around when I noticed a guy on his own coming our way. He was tan with broad shoulders, blond hair combed back and neatly parted, a crisp mustache, and a blue suit with an unbuttoned white shirt under it. He looked as though he was just out of school but trying to look older.

"Excuse me, ladies, are these seats taken?" he asked, green eyes sparkling as he pointed at the two seats Aaron and I had been sitting in.

Mom looked up at him. Millie did the same, her jaw hanging open as he flashed her a smile.

"They're ours," Aaron replied before either of them had a chance to answer. He pulled my chair out for me and quickly sat in the other one.

The guy held his palms out. "My apologies. I didn't mean any offense," he said. "I'll leave you to your—"

"I'm sure we can find another chair some-where," Millie broke in. She scanned the room and pointed at the table next to ours. "Look, there's an extra one there. I'm sure they won't mind if you borrow it."

"Only if you're sure. I don't want to intrude. I just saw a couple of beautiful ladies and couldn't believe your husbands had left you alone."

Aaron looked at me and made a face. I stifled a laugh.

"I'm single!" Millie trilled. "Come on. Grab that chair. We can all fit."

A moment later the guy was back with the chair, which he proceeded to squeeze into the gap between Mom and Millie.

"That's better," Millie said once we'd all shuffled around to let him in and introduced ourselves.

"I'm Noah," he said. "I must say, it's kind of you to let me join you. I'm here on business, and it's rather lonely when you're traveling solo."

"I know how you feel," Mom said wistfully.

Noah turned to her. "You're single too?" he asked, raising an eyebrow. "I refuse to believe that!"

Mom laughed as her cheeks reddened. "My husband is . . ."

"My dad's on business too," I cut in. "We'll be back with him soon. Very soon." I wasn't going to let an overgrown teenager try to make a move on Mom. Yuck!

"Thank you, Emily. I can speak for myself," Mom snapped. She turned back to Noah. "What was I saying?"

Noah smiled at Mom. "I *think* you were saying that your husband is away and there's nothing to stop me from having the pleasure of a beautiful woman's company for the evening."

Millie coughed loudly. Noah twisted in his seat to face her. "The pleasure of *two* beautiful women's company," he added quickly.

I glanced at Aaron and rolled my eyes as Millie flicked her hair and blushed.

"What business are you in?" Aaron asked.

"Diamonds," Noah answered quickly. Then he turned back to Mom. "And might I say, I couldn't help noticing your stunning necklace."

Mom reached up to her neck. "It was a gift from my husband," she said. "He gave it to me so I wouldn't feel alone."

Noah put a hand to his chest. "Oh, I love a bit of romance." Then he got up. "Well," he said, "if your husband isn't here to object, I shall have to dance with you." He pushed his chair back and held a hand out to Mom. "Come on. Please," he said. "Take pity on a lonely traveler."

As Mom stood up, Noah turned to Millie. "Promise you'll dance with me next?" he asked.

Millie shrugged. "Maybe. Unless I get a better offer."

Noah took Mom's arm and they made their way to the dance floor.

"Is that guy for real?" Aaron asked through his teeth as Millie got her makeup bag out and started reapplying her lipstick.

"I hope so," she replied as she pursed her lips into her compact mirror. "He's hot."

Aaron and I looked at each other and burst out laughing.

"What?"

"Millie, he's probably half your age!" I said.

Millie shrugged. "So what?" she asked. "Nothing wrong with a bit of flirting and a dance or two, is there?"

We watched Mom and Noah for a while. Noah was a good dancer—apart from one point when he suddenly jumped back from Mom as if he'd tripped over something.

Aaron nudged me. "Looks like he's got two left feet, like me," he said with a laugh.

Just then, the song finished. "OK, folks, we're going to slow things down a little," the singer said. "Who knows how to waltz?"

A cheer went up in the far corner and some of the older couples got up and made their way onto the dance floor.

"Shall we give it a try?" Aaron asked.

"A waltz? Are you serious?" I asked.

Aaron shrugged. "Why not?"

"Didn't you bump into me enough times during the chicken dance?" I joked.

"Hey!"

I turned to Millie. "Do you mind? Will you be OK on your own?"

Millie jabbed her thumb at the dance floor. "Oh, I won't be alone for long," she said. "It's my turn next."

"All right, then," I said, and followed Aaron to the dance floor.

When the music started, we tried to dance in time but didn't do a good job of it. "OK, I officially hate the waltz!" Aaron declared once the song ended. "Please, let's promise *never* to try doing it again."

I laughed. "If I ever want to use my toes again, I think that's a good plan."

The band was still playing slow tunes, so we stayed on the dance floor and just kind of swayed together to the music.

"Are you having a good time?" Aaron asked as he slipped his arms around my waist.

"Of course I am. It's amazing," I said. "Are you?"

"Yeah," he said. "I guess."

I pulled away so I could look at him. "You *guess*? I thought you'd love this trip."

"I do. The ship's amazing," he said. "And I can't wait to check out the rides on the top deck tomorrow. Just. Well . . . us."

I leaned my head on his shoulder. "Yeah," I said.

"I'm going to miss you, that's all," Aaron said. "After this trip, Mom and I will be getting ready to leave, and then that's it. I mean, I want to go and live on Forgotten Island. But, you know."

He didn't need to explain. I knew what he meant.

"Aaron," I said carefully. "Do you think we should . . . ?"

I didn't want to finish the sentence. I couldn't bring myself to say the thoughts out loud.

"We should what?" Aaron asked.

"Well, with you going to live somewhere else. Maybe it's not fair that you feel tied down. You should be free to go off and do your thing without worrying about me."

This time it was Aaron's turn to pull away from me. He held my arms. "Emily, are you breaking up with me?" he asked. "You want us to split up? Is that what you're saying?"

Was it? *Did* I want us to break up? I was so busy trying to figure out what would be the right thing for Aaron I hadn't even stopped to think about what might actually be best for *me*. One look at Aaron's face told me that now wasn't the time to start thinking about it.

"No," I said. "Of course that's not what I'm saying."

"You're sure?"

"I just don't want to be selfish," I mumbled. "Holding you back. If you want to break up, I guess I just wanted you to know that it's OK to say so."

Aaron grinned as he put his arms around me again. "You're not being selfish and you're not holding me back," he said. "And I *don't* want us to break up," he said. "Unless you do."

"No," I replied. "Unless *you* do."

Aaron laughed. "Good. That's settled." He took my hand and led me off the dance floor. "Come on. I need a drink."

Mom had come back from the dance floor, too, and was chatting with Millie. Noah had gone over to the bar. "I haven't danced like that in years!" Mom said as we joined them at the table. "It was quite exhilarating."

"Mmm, I suppose it must have been," Millie said tightly as a young guy who couldn't have looked more different from Noah lumbered across the room. I couldn't help watching him — he looked so out of place. He was wearing a ragged T-shirt and ripped jeans, and his hair looked like it hadn't been brushed in a lifetime; it was sticking up in every direction.

He tripped over a chair leg at the edge of the dance floor and nearly landed in an elderly man's trifle. "Sorry, sorry," he muttered, patting the man's arm to check if he was OK.

The man flicked the boy's hand away, as if swatting a fly. I couldn't help feeling sorry for him. Yeah, he was a bit scruffy, but the way people were looking at him, you'd think he was radioactive or something.

As he crossed the dance floor, I noticed him look down at the floor and stop walking. He glanced around, then bent down to pick something up. I couldn't see what it was as there were still people dancing and he went out of sight. When he straightened up, he glanced around again, then put his hand in his pocket before carrying on walking. He sauntered in our direction.

As he came toward us, I smiled. I didn't want him thinking everyone in the place was a snob who looked down on him just because he might not be dressed as nicely as them.

He gave me a rueful half smile back and walked past us.

"Want some more dessert?" Aaron asked.

I laughed. "Aren't you full?"

"The dancing is working it off," he replied.

"Good point," I said, getting up from my seat. "Maybe a bit more chocolate fondue."

"And maybe one last bowl of mint chocolate-chip ice cream," Aaron added as we got up from our seats. "Anyone else want anything?"

"Could you fetch me a strawberry meringue tartlet?" Millie asked.

"Will do."

The scruffy boy was in front of us at the buffet table. As we lined up behind him, he picked up a plate.

I watched him pile it high.

"You having some sort of contest?" I asked, laughing.

He turned sharply, his eyes glaring at me. They were piercing blue. "What do you mean?" he snapped. "Who said I'm having a contest?"

I held my palms out in front of me. "Hey, chill," I said. "I just meant . . . *that.*" I pointed at the people in front of him in the line, plates piled with food almost as high as his. "It was a joke."

The boy smiled. "Sorry, I didn't mean to be rude," he said. Then he glanced at his plate and laughed. "And, yeah, good point. I do have quite a bit, don't I?"

Aaron leaned over my shoulder. "Don't worry," he said. "We'll probably end up with just as much ourselves."

The boy laughed. "OK, start again?" he said. "I'm Sam. Nice to meet you."

"I'm Emily."

"And I'm Aaron. Emily's *boyfriend,*" Aaron said pointedly. Not that Sam noticed the emphasis. He was more focused on carefully holding his marshmallow under the fondue so every bit got covered in chocolate.

"You having a good vacation?" I asked.

Sam looked at me quizzically. "Huh?"

That was when it occurred to me. Perhaps

he wasn't on vacation. Maybe he worked on the ship, in maintenance or something. He might have come fresh from fixing something. That would explain why he looked so out of place.

"Oh. Do you work on the ship?" I asked.

"I — no, well, yes, I . . ."

I laughed. "OK, whatever," I said. I grabbed a couple of cookies and looked around for the strawberry meringue tartlets for Millie.

"My dad," the boy was still mumbling. "He's, um . . . he's quite important. So, that's why . . . you know. That's why I'm here."

I found the tartlets and put one on my plate for Millie. "He's important, is he? What is he, like, the captain?" I asked, joking.

Sam put a thumbnail in his mouth and chewed on it while he thought. It wasn't really a difficult question. Either his dad was the captain of the ship or not. What was there to think about?

"Yeah," he said eventually. "My dad's the boss." Then he turned away.

And before I had time to say anything else, he'd disappeared across the room.

I turned back to Aaron. "Well, that was weird," I said, laughing.

"Very," Aaron agreed. His face was serious.

I squeezed his arm. "Aaron, you don't need to be jealous," I said. "He's only —"

"I'm not jealous," Aaron said. "That's not it."

"What, then? Why the serious face?"

Aaron's eyes were following Sam as he spoke. "Because I chatted to the captain for a bit when we were at that reception before dinner," he said.

"And?"

Aaron was still looking away. "And I told him how cool I thought all the gadgets were. I said I bet his kids loved coming on the ship to visit."

I waited. Aaron carried on staring across the room. "And know what he said?"

"What?"

"He laughed and agreed his children *would* love it. But he doesn't have any, so he wouldn't know." Aaron turned to me. "Emily, Sam was lying. The captain doesn't have a son."

Which left two questions. Who on earth *was* Sam, and why had he lied to us?

Chapter Three

"Don't look now," Mom said, nudging Millie. "But I think someone is heading our way."

A moment later, Noah appeared at our table. He was holding two drinks. Handing one to Mom, he placed the other on the table and then held his arm out for Millie. "Apologies for the delay," he said. "Two mojitos, with an extra twist of lime. Hope I've got that right."

Mom raised an eyebrow. "Well, you're observant, aren't you?"

"I try my best," Noah replied. Then he turned to Millie. "You can drink yours after the next dance."

Millie took a couple of sips of her drink. "Well, if you *insist*," she said as she got out of her seat.

We watched them dance for a bit. At the end of the song, the lead singer spoke over the mic. "We're going to take a short break now. See you all again soon."

Noah and Millie came back to the table. Millie didn't look impressed.

"One dance," she complained as a woman in ship's uniform approached our table. She had a stack of papers in her hands.

"Evening, folks," she said with a bright smile. "Can I give you one of these?"

"What are they?" Mom asked as the woman handed her a sheet of paper.

"The *Sunbeam* quiz," the woman replied. "Just a bit of fun for you while the band takes a break. First correct set of answers wins a prize." She reached into her pocket and put a pencil on the table. "Good luck!" she trilled as she moved on to the next table.

Noah was fiddling with a napkin. After pulling it out of the ring, he wiped his mouth then scrunched it up and put it back down on the table. He rummaged in his pockets as if he were searching for something, then he leaned forward to get out of his chair. "Well, I'll leave you to—" he began.

"No you won't," Millie replied sharply, tugging on his sleeve. "You can help."

I stifled a laugh, and so did Aaron. Noah glanced across at us and raised his eyebrows as he smiled. Maybe he wasn't so bad, after all.

"Your brain might be handy," Millie went on. "Come on. Gather around folks. Let's see if we can win the prize."

"OK, go for it," Mom said.

"Right." Millie cleared her throat. "Question one. *Travel awhile through the mist, if you will. You may find a king on this semi-dark hill.*"

Millie stared around at us all. "What in the name of the goddess is that supposed to mean?" she asked.

"It's a cryptic clue," Mom said.

"You're not wrong there," I agreed.

Aaron leaned in to whisper his answer. "It's Halflight Castle."

Of course! Halflight Castle was where Aaron had spent most of his life, until he came to live in Brightport this year. One of the reasons his mom had agreed to try living at Forgotten Island was because it was near to her old home.

Noah stroked his mustache. "Impressive," he

said, appraising Aaron as he leaned back in his seat. "How did you know that?"

"I used to live there," Aaron said.

Noah almost fell forward as he straightened his chair. "You *what*? You lived at Halflight Castle?"

"Yep. For more than thirteen years. Have you heard of it?"

Noah nodded. For a moment, his smooth facade seemed to have disappeared and he looked different. Younger, and more like the excited teenager he probably was.

"My dad told us about it just before—before we—I—left," he stammered. "I've been trying to find out more. I guess you know the area around here pretty well."

"I know enough," Aaron said. "What I haven't seen in real life, I know from my old bedroom at the castle."

"How's that?" Noah asked.

"I used to have stuff all over my walls."

"Stuff?" Noah's eyes were wide. "What kind of stuff did you have on your walls?"

Aaron shrugged. "Maps, diagrams, pictures— I used to study it all."

Noah seemed to have recovered himself a bit; he slowly nodded. "Well, I take my hat off to you," he said. "I'm impressed. Very impressed."

Aaron tried to suppress a smile. Even *he* was falling under Noah's spell now.

"OK, next question," Millie said.

"Sorry, guys," Noah said suddenly. Something across the room seemed to have caught his attention. "Got to go."

"You can't leave," Millie protested. "We've only just—"

"I'd love to, but duty calls," he interrupted. "Well done again, Aaron," he said. "I'll be keeping my eye on you."

For some reason, his words made me shiver.

I didn't get to think about it for long. A moment later, Noah pushed his chair back, got out of his seat, and left.

"Well, I—" Millie began.

"Come on. Never mind him. What's the next question?" I asked. "With Aaron's brain on the case, I think we might have a chance of winning this."

We put our heads together and worked our way through the rest of the quiz.

Twenty minutes later, the quiz was over. Greta said they'd be announcing the winners later. In the meantime, the music had started up again.

I took Aaron's hand. "I'm ready for another dance. You coming?"

"Sure." Aaron said as he followed me to the dance floor.

We'd been dancing for a couple of songs, goofing off and laughing just like earlier, when the music suddenly stopped.

The band looked as shocked as the rest of us. They were still on the stage—still playing their instruments—but there was no sound coming out.

The lead singer tapped his mic. Nothing.

"Sorry, folks, technical hitch," he called to the room. "We'll hopefully be up and running again soon."

His voice was drowned out by a screeching sound over the loudspeaker.

And then—

"I'm afraid you won't!" a deep, gruff voice announced.

Where had that come from?

"Ladies and gentlemen," the voice went on. "Your evening plans have changed. Return to your seats and wait for more information."

"Who's that?" "What's he saying?" "What's going on?" People were muttering everywhere.

The loudspeaker screeched again, and then the voice bellowed. "Return to your seats NOW! In

33

case I wasn't clear, this is not a request. It is an order. And for those asking who I am . . ."

The room was silent for a beat and then the voice spoke again. This time he didn't need to bellow. His words were almost a whisper.

"I am now the man in charge."

All around, people turned to one another, asking questions, gesturing, shaking their heads.

"I think we should do what the man says and go back to our seats," Aaron said.

"I agree."

We joined Mom and Millie at our table. Mom had turned white. "What's going on?" she asked.

I shrugged. "No idea." I looked around and couldn't see a single person in ship's uniform. What had happened to them all?

Millie pulled her shawl tighter around her. "'Man in charge' indeed," she said with a sniff. "I'll give him 'man in charge.'" She started to get out of her seat.

"Let's just wait and see what's going to happen, OK, Mills?" Mom replied, holding an arm out to stop her. "Let's not do anything hasty."

Most people had returned to their seats, a lot of them grumbling and complaining as they did so.

And then someone looked out a porthole.

It was an older man with white hair and a dark-blue suit with medals on his lapel. "Hey! Look at this!" he shouted. A few of the people making their way back to their tables stopped and looked where he was pointing.

It was like a ripple effect. Each of the people looking out called to someone else. One by one, people were getting up from their seats, ignoring the orders, and making their way to the portholes along the far side of the ship.

The more people who looked out, the more gasps carried across the room.

I was halfway out of my chair. "I'm going to see what's going on," I said.

"Emily, don't," Mom replied. "You heard what he said. We have to stay in our seats."

I waved a hand around the room. "Mom, look. Everyone's getting up to see what it is. Whoever the man is, he can't stop us if we *all* go."

"Emily's right," Millie said as she pulled herself out of her seat. "I want to see what's happening too. Come on. Safety in numbers."

So the four of us crossed the room together. We got as close to the nearest window as we could. It was hard, as people were piling up in front of them now.

We looked in the direction people were pointing. And then we saw it.

A huge ship—at least half the length of our cruise ship. It looked like it had four masts, with lines of gleaming white sails on each one. A long golden pole sticking out at the front—the bowsprit—had three more sails on it.

Looking farther out to sea, I could just about make out the shapes of a couple of other ships that seemed to be heading toward us too.

People were pointing and muttering to each other as we all stared. A murmur started to go through the crowd. What were they saying? Something about a flag.

I scanned the ship from front to back.

And then I saw it. A black background with a smiling skull and, below it, a pair of bones crossed over each other.

I couldn't speak. My mouth had gone dry. I knew exactly what we were looking at.

A pirate ship.

"I believe I told you all to take your seats!" The voice boomed over the speakers again. "I haven't got all night."

I glanced around the room as we made our way back to our seats. Where was the voice coming from? And who was it? Whoever it was, he was sounding more impatient each time he spoke.

Finally, everyone was back at their tables. There was a rustling sound at the front of the room, and then someone walked onto the stage.

He was wearing a sandy-colored shirt with a brown leather vest over it that hung loosely over baggy trousers. Medals or badges or something lined his lapels. His ruddy red face looked as worn as his vest, and his black hair was tied back in a ponytail. He had a narrow beard that stretched in a line from his bottom lip and dangled down below the bottom of his chin. Lining his top lip, he sported a mustache that twirled out beyond each cheek. He looked as though he'd just walked off the set of an old-fashioned kids' film about pirates.

For a moment, I wondered if this was actually part of the ship's entertainment.

"Good evening, ladies and gents," the man said. It was the same voice that had been giving us instructions. "I hate to spoil your evening . . ." He paused for a second before adding, "Actually, who am I kidding? I LOVE to spoil your evening!" He burst out laughing. A nasty, evil, throaty laugh that sent shivers through me. OK, this was starting to feel a little too real now.

As abruptly as it had started, the laughing stopped.

"What? You don't find my jokes funny?" he asked as he stared around the room. The roomful of people responded by staring silently back at him.

"Well, never mind," he went on, flicking a hand as if to shake us off. "I'm not too bothered about whether you have a sense of humor. I'm more interested in whether you have any valuable possessions." He burst out laughing again, then scanned the room. "Looks like there's probably a fair bit of money in this place."

As he spoke, people instinctively reached down to pull their bags and purses closer. They folded down sleeves to cover expensive watches, reached up to their necks to hide necklaces under their tops.

I noticed Mom do the same. She fumbled around on her neck. Then she turned to me. "Emily!" she hissed. "I can't feel my necklace."

I studied her neck and shook my head. "Mom! It's gone!" I whispered back.

Mom swallowed. "It *can't* be gone," she whispered. Her eyes had turned glassy with tears.

"You probably just dropped it while you were dancing. We'll look for it as soon as he's finished. We'll find it."

"Anyway. I'm being very rude," the man went on. "I haven't even introduced myself." He waited a beat. The room was silent; it felt as though every single person was holding their breath while we waited for him to go on.

"I," he said, pausing dramatically, "am the pirate king."

Finally, the room had again hushed enough for the pirate king to continue. "I'll tell you what's going to happen next," he said. "It won't take long, and if you all behave impeccably then no one will be hurt. My family and I are simply here to relieve you of—well, basically, anything we want."

The pirate king laughed again. At least he found his own jokes funny, though no one else did. The roomful of people stared at him in silent fear. I could feel my heart thud harder in my chest every time he spoke. Questions were flying around and around in my head. What was he going to do with us? Would we ever get home? Had he stolen Mom's necklace?

"A little bit of housekeeping before we go any further." The pirate king interrupted my internal questions.

"Just in case you get ideas above your station and think you can take us on, I should make it clear that I have taken *complete* control of the ship. The captain and his senior crew have been taken hostage in the wheelhouse and my men are now operating the ship from the bridge. I have lookouts on every deck. If anyone so much as makes a move to challenge me or my men, your captain and his crew will *suffer the consequences.*"

The pirate king paused to let his words sink in. The look on his face showed us that this was no empty threat. The silent looks he got in reply showed that we all knew it. "Good," he drawled. "Now that that's settled, let's get down to business. I sent my sons ahead of me. A sort of advance party, if you will. Let's get them up onstage, shall we?"

He cupped his hand over his eyes as he scanned the room. "First of all, let's have my oldest, the apple of my eye. Where are you, son?"

Behind me, I heard a scraping of chairs as someone came forward from the back of the room.

He wove through the tables, came past us, and made his way to the stage.

No! Surely not!

The pirate king's older son stepped up onto the stage and turned to smile at the room.

We'd spent half the evening looking at that smile.

The charming, polite guy who'd worked the room, danced with Mom and Millie, even managed to draw Aaron and me under his spell.

Noah was the pirate king's son!

He beamed at the room, smiling as if he were a talk-show host or something. "I believe I've met some of you already," he said. He scanned the room, giving a wave here and there. When his eyes fell on our table, he winked and blew a kiss.

All that talk, all that smooth charm, and he was a nasty, scheming pirate! I could barely believe what I was seeing.

"Why, that's—" Millie began. "That's . . ." She was so flustered she couldn't even finish her sentence. Sputtering, she pointed at Noah, jabbing her finger at him as she turned around to me. "It's—"

"Leave it, Millie. We don't want to draw attention to ourselves," Mom said as she put a hand on Millie's arm. Her face was pinched and tight.

The pirate king looked into the crowd. "Now, let's get my younger lad up, shall we? Where are you, son?"

A moment later, a scruffy boy stumbled onto the stage, pulling his hair out of his eyes as he joined his brother and dad.

No way!

It was Sam! The guy we'd talked to at the buffet. The one who disappeared. No wonder he'd acted so strangely!

Sam stood beside his big brother, staring down at the floor as he scuffed his feet.

"My sons and I will shortly be on the move," the pirate king announced. "But first, I've been in this game long enough to know what you want. You want to know how quickly you can get out of here and whether you'll live to tell the tale." He laughed again, as if everything he said was so hilarious. "So, I'll tell you. Yes, you'll all get out of here alive—as long as you do what you're told, that is. And I suppose the quicker my crew fills five bags up with gold, jewels, and money, the sooner we'll be off."

A low grumble went around the room.

He took a step forward, right up to the front of the stage, and flashed an exaggerated pretend smile. "Any questions?"

Silence.

"OK, then. I have assigned my crew to each section of the room. They will escort you to your cabins, and you will do exactly as they say."

42

The pirate king surveyed us one last time. "Remember, do exactly what they tell you and everyone will be happy." He pointed at his sons. "You two, stay here. We have work to do."

And with that, the pirate king and his sons climbed down from the stage and chose a table to sit at, while the pirates who had been waiting around the edges of the room began their task of escorting us back to our cabins.

One of the pirates indicated for us to get out of our seats. "Come on," he said. "My boss doesn't like to be kept waiting. Let's get moving."

We made our way to the edge of the room with everyone else. Once we were through the doors, people spilled out into the corridor. The pirate king's crew barked orders every now and then, but it was still quite a chaotic crush.

Which is probably why it took me till we'd gotten all the way back to our rooms before I realized something.

Aaron had disappeared.

Chapter Four

*A*s we approached our rooms, we had to slow down because there was a bit of a bottleneck. I took the opportunity to have a good look around. Mom and Millie were ahead. A couple I recognized from the dance floor was on one side of me; a family with two young kids and a baby were on the other.

People were squashed into every bit of space in the corridor, and I scanned them all. No Aaron. He'd disappeared, definitely.

I felt something unpleasant flutter in my stomach. No. I didn't need to get scared. There was a rational explanation; there had to be. Maybe he'd gotten lost, or gone to the bathroom, or . . .

Or *what*? I couldn't come up with a good reason for him to have simply disappeared. He *never* did anything like that.

OK, I needed a strategy. First, calm down. Second, make absolutely, totally, one hundred percent sure he wasn't here. Then, and only then, panic.

I slowed my walk, letting others push past me, till I was right at the back of the crowd.

The pirate guy who was escorting us to our cabins had been joined by another one. The two of them were talking about something. I hung back farther so I could listen in.

"He's done what?" our pirate was asking.

"He's taken him," the other one replied. "Noah pointed him out and told me and Jonny to take care of it. Jonny's got him now. I've got to get back to the ballroom and report in to Noah."

"Right. OK."

As the other pirate turned to leave, he caught my eye. "What do you want, little girl?"

"Nothing!" I said quickly.

He nodded slowly. "Good. Keep it that way." Then he mimed pulling a zipper across his mouth. "And keep that shut too," he added with a snarl.

I could feel my face burning. Partly out of embarrassment at being caught listening in on their conversation, but more because what I'd heard had confirmed my worst fears. The pirates had taken someone, and Aaron had gone missing. Even if I didn't know *why* Noah would want to snatch him, I knew in my heart that he had.

I wormed my way forward into the crowd, away from the pirate at the back. I tried to make myself invisible, ducking down and finding the busiest part of the group. To my left and just ahead of me, I noticed a door in the wall. I maneuvered myself so I was near the edge of the corridor. As I got closer, I could see the door had a sign that said STAFF CLEANING on it. Shuffling along at this rate, I'd reach the door in about a minute.

I quickly hatched a plan.

I would sneak through the door, wait in the cleaning closet till everyone had passed by, then creep out again and get away. Once the coast was clear, I'd retrace our steps back to the ballroom to see if I could find out what had happened to Aaron.

We edged forward a tiny bit. I was beside the door. Without looking at it, I ran my hand down

46

the door till I found the handle. I twisted the doorknob one way. Nothing happened. Then the other. I felt something click. Pushing my weight gently against the door, I felt it give. Yes! It was unlocked.

I pretended to fiddle with my hair so I could sneak another look around. The pirate was still at the back, talking to one of the guests.

This was it. I glanced around one more time to make sure no one was watching—and then I pushed the door open and slid inside.

I softly closed the door behind me and held my breath while I listened to the people shuffle by on the other side of the door. Then I heard the pirate's voice. "Come on. Keep moving. Stop dawdling. You, yes, you, back there. Move it."

He was right outside!

My heart was thudding so loud I was afraid he would hear it, even through the door.

The shuffling carried on for a few more minutes. Then . . . silence. Everyone had gone.

I'd done it. I'd gotten away!

Finally allowing myself to calm down, I leaned against the door and counted to one hundred.

Coming, ready or not.

I opened the door a tiny crack. Barely breathing, I slowly opened it farther, wide enough so I could poke my head out.

The corridor was empty.

Without stopping to think about it, I sneaked out of the closet and ran back in the direction we'd come.

I retraced our steps all the way back to the ballroom, checking around every corner, peeking into every nook and cranny, calling out Aaron's name in a whisper, on the off chance that he'd gotten away and was hiding somewhere.

Nothing. The corridors were deserted.

I reached the ballroom. What if he was in there with the pirates? I couldn't exactly march through the main door and demand they hand him over. I'd have to find another way in. Maybe a back entrance where I could sneak in and at least cast my eyes over the room without being detected.

I followed the corridor till I found a door that said STAFF ONLY in big letters.

Bingo.

I pushed the door open as slowly and silently as I could and squeezed inside.

I was in an empty kitchen. All around me, shiny metal surfaces were covered in dirty dishes, used cutlery, food that hadn't been put away. The staff had been caught by surprise, just like the rest of us.

I could hear muffled voices coming from the ballroom. They were still out there. I crept across the kitchen to the far side. I had to get somewhere I could observe them from more closely. A pair of heavy swinging doors were closed. I couldn't risk opening them; they'd hear me. There must be somewhere else.

I found it at the far end of the kitchen. There was a sliding door that, if I'd calculated correctly, led to the far end of the ballroom, near the stage. It was half open.

I crept up to the door, shimmied sideways through the gap, and poked my head out to look.

I was right. The stage was ahead of me — but there was a gap between the door and the stage that went straight out to the main room. I couldn't risk running out of here. The pirate king and his two sons were sitting at a table in front of the stage.

They were about twenty steps away from me and completely oblivious to the fact that I was there.

My heart sank. Three pirates. No Aaron.

Someone else was coming into the ballroom!

The three pirates looked up as the door at the far end of the room opened. This was my chance. I could run across to the stage while they were all looking the other way. Maybe Aaron was there, with the other pirate. Jonny, or whatever he was called.

I probably had a two-second window while they were looking away. So I darted across the gap and made it to the stage. I hid behind a curtain and listened.

"Sir, your wife is here," a voice called from the other side of the ballroom. "Shall I tell her you'll join her after your meeting?"

"No! bring her in," the pirate king replied.

"Yes, sir."

I heard the door close again and a chair scrape back.

"All right, sons," the pirate king was saying. "I hope you are going to make your mother happy. You know how she feels about these business trips, so I'm depending on you to help me make it worth her while. You hear me?"

"Yes, Father," the two boys replied in unison.

Just hearing their voices made a dart of anger scratch through my chest.

I didn't get to dwell on it for long, as I heard the door open again and a flurry of people come into the room.

Voices coming closer.

While they were distracted by greeting each other, I pulled the curtain a little farther out, so I could get into a better position for listening in on their conversation, to see if they revealed anything that might help me find Aaron. Now I could see a little from my hiding place too.

At the far end of the ballroom, a woman had entered and was striding across to meet them.

She was as tall as the pirate king and as outlandishly dressed. She wore a black dress with a purple jacket over it. Her hair was orange, her ears held the biggest earrings I'd ever seen, and her neck had so many gold necklaces around it I was surprised she could take the weight of them.

It didn't take much to figure out that this was the pirate king's wife.

As she approached her husband and sons, the three of them got up from their seats. The pirate king kissed her cheek and pulled a chair back for her, before all four of them sat down.

"My darling, how do you like our little excursion?" the pirate king asked.

His wife flicked back her hair. "Ask me when they bring me the spoils," she replied haughtily. "I really cannot judge till then." She cast her eyes around the room. "I suppose it looks fine enough."

"It does, my dear, it does," the pirate king

replied. "And speaking of finery and spoils, I have organized a surprise for you," he went on. "I thought I'd spice things up with a little competition. The boys were given the task of fetching something for you while they were scoping out the ship for me. I told them you'd choose your favorite."

His wife tutted and shook her head. "You boys," she muttered. "Always with the competitions."

The pirate king turned to his sons. I ducked back behind the curtain, as he was almost directly facing me, but I could still just about see around the edge.

"I believe you each have something for your mother," the pirate king said. He was looking almost directly toward me. I stopped breathing and prayed that my shape wasn't visible through the curtain. "The winner is the one whose gift she prefers. Noah, let's start with you."

Noah cleared his throat as he reached into his jacket pocket. "Now, Mother, I would normally give you something much, much better than this," he began. For the first time since we'd met him, he seemed awkward and uncertain. "But time was limited and—"

"Enough talk, son," his father chided him. "Just give your mother her gift."

Noah pulled his hand out of his pocket and opened it.

His mom took an object from Noah's palm and examined it. As she held it up, I could see it was silver and round.

"You got me a *napkin ring*?" his mother announced in a voice that even from this distance didn't sound impressed. To be fair, I'm not sure *I* would have been impressed with a napkin ring either.

She held it up to examine it more closely. "I suppose it *is* shiny," she went on, squinting against the light. It sounded like she was desperately trying to find something positive to say about it.

As Noah's mom continued to study the napkin ring, I realized I recognized it. We'd had them at the tables. For all I knew, that was what he'd been up to when he was shuffling around with his napkin. Stealing a napkin ring from our table!

The pirate king stared at his oldest son. His face had turned bright red. "Noah, I expected better from you," he growled.

"I'm sorry. I—I tried to get something else. It was beautiful. It was perfect, but it slipped through my fingers and then I lost it and—"

"Enough!" His dad cut him off. "No excuses." He nodded at Sam. "Well, son? Here's your chance. Let's see if you can do better than your brother."

"For once," Noah muttered.

His mom tutted at Noah and smacked his hand.

"Now, now," she said. Then she smiled fondly at Sam. "What have you gotten me, darling boy?" she asked in a voice about fifty times softer than she'd used up to now.

Sam fumbled in his pocket and held something up.

It was too small to see exactly what it was from here. They were all staring at it, so I risked edging forward a bit to see better. I pushed the curtain and leaned out as far as I dared.

"I got you this, Mother," Sam said.

As I shifted position, and Sam continued to hold his gift out, I saw what it was. I had to clamp a hand over my mouth to stop myself from gasping out loud and giving myself away.

A chain. Fine, shiny gold, with a pendant on it. Two interlocked hearts—one made of tiny diamonds, the other gold. A mermaid's tail looped around the hearts.

Sam's present to his mother—it was my mom's necklace!

Chapter Five

O h, Sam," his mom exclaimed. "It's beautiful. So fine. So delicate."

"Nice work, son," the pirate king agreed, stroking his beard as he nodded approvingly.

Nice work? *Nice work?*

I could barely hold myself back. I wanted to storm down there and snatch the necklace out of their greedy, thieving hands.

But then, suddenly, everything changed.

The pirate king leaned forward to take a closer look. As he did, his face darkened. "Wait a minute," he growled. "Samuel, what is the meaning of this?"

"Of what, Father?" Sam asked.

The pirate king pointed at the necklace with a shaking hand. "That *thing* on this necklace. It's a—it's a—I can't even say it!"

Sam examined the necklace more closely, as if he were properly looking at it for the first time. His cheeks reddened.

Noah looked over his brother's shoulder to see what they were studying. For a split second, his eyes flashed with something that looked like recognition or shock. Then he scowled. "A mermaid!" he exclaimed. His face was full of disgust. "You got Mom a necklace with a *mermaid* on it? Seriously?" He burst out laughing. "Oh, man, you are priceless," he said, slapping his brother on the back.

"How could you do such a thing?" the pirate king growled. "Everyone knows that mermaids are bad luck. Even the toughest of pirates fear them. *This* is how you show us what you think of us? *This* is how much respect you have for me? *This* is how little you think of your mother, that you'd give her a mermaid necklace?"

"Father, I hadn't realized—" Sam began.

His dad waved an arm to stop him and continued his tirade. "Do you not remember your history, son? Or do you simply not care about it?"

"Neither! Father, I—"

"I banned mermaids from being so much as *talked* about after one of them lured your grandfather toward dangerous rocks that broke up his ship and nearly killed him. And then you insult your mother like this." He hissed in disgust.

I could barely believe what I was hearing. It felt like they had reached inside of me, pulled my insides out to examine them, and then thrown them away, repelled.

The pirate king's wife had leaned forward to look more closely at the necklace. As she did, her face turned gray.

"Get that thing away from me!" she shrieked. "Get it out of my sight! Put it in one of the bags with the rest of the takings from this ship. Just don't let me see it again!"

"You heard your mother," the pirate king said. "Get rid of it."

"I'm sorry," Sam said as he shoved the necklace back in his pocket. His voice sounded forlorn and miserable, like a little boy desperate to please his parents but resigned to failing.

The pirate king turned to Noah. "Under the circumstances, I have no option but to declare you the winner of round one. Not a great win, but a win nevertheless."

Noah threw back his chair as he practically

bounced out of it. He slapped his brother on the back so hard that Sam almost fell forward onto the table. Then he made a fist and punched the air. "Bad luck, bro," he crowed. "I win. As usual."

"All right, Noah," his mother said. "No need to rub it in."

"Why not?" her husband asked. "These boys are out there representing *me*. It's my family business, my name on the letterhead, my name Sam makes a mockery of with stunts like this. Your babying him doesn't help any of us."

His wife took a sharp breath in. "My *what*?"

The pirate king opened his mouth. Nothing came out of it for a moment. Then in a placative voice, he said, "I—I mean, not that you *baby* him, exactly. You're a wonderful mother, Michele. The best."

Michele folded her arms and raised an eyebrow.

"I just mean—come on, the boy needs to toughen up. Remember whose family he's part of."

"*Our* family, Jakob," she said. "Ours, not yours. And *I* say don't be so hard on him."

The pirate king let a breath whistle out through his gold teeth. "All right, all right. Let's move on." He turned back to his sons. "Here's the plan," he said, leaning on the table. "My crew will be busy all night collecting goods. In that time, we need to get ready for the main challenge."

"The main challenge?" Sam asked.

His father glared at him. "Yes, son. Round one was the warm-up. There are two more rounds to go. Think you're up to a serious test of your abilities?"

"Of course I am!"

"Good. Well, then, this is your chance to prove it." He sat back in his seat. "If you win round two, you're even with your brother, and you might earn back some of the respect you've thrown in my face with this stunt."

He pulled something out of his pocket, and he and his sons leaned over to look at it. What was it? I needed to be nearer.

Could I risk pushing the curtain aside? Would it be obvious?

I took the chance. Pushing gently on the curtain, I edged slowly forward. They'd unfolded a large sheet that they were leaning over and studying. It looked like it could be a map. Probably a sea chart.

"This is where we are right now," the pirate king was saying. He prodded the chart. "You remember before we got here, I gave you the names of some important local landmarks and told you to learn all you could about this area?"

"Certainly do, Father," Noah replied. He was smirking as if he had a big secret that he was desperate to share. "Like Halflight Castle?"

59

"Well remembered, son," his father replied. "You have tonight to become as familiar as possible with the area. In the morning, you will use your knowledge, your skills, your crew, and your instincts to compete in round two."

Noah was practically bouncing out of his seat.

"What is it, son?" Jakob snapped. "Why are you so antsy?"

"No reason," Noah replied with a massive grin. "Just that I've used my initiative to seize the advantage already." Then, as if he'd just told the funniest joke, he burst out laughing. "Ha — get it? *Seized* the advantage. Literally!"

My ears pricked up. What was he saying?

Sam echoed my thoughts. "What are you talking about?" he grumbled.

"I'll give you a clue," his brother taunted him. "Let's say I've enlisted a willing helper. Well, maybe not *willing,* as such. But when it comes to local knowledge, all I'll say is that you might as well give up now, bro."

A willing helper.

Local knowledge.

I knew exactly what Noah was saying. I prayed and wished and hoped as hard as I could that I was wrong.

And then Noah went on. "All right, then. I'll

tell you. Found myself a local guy. He knows the area inside out."

I shoved my fist into my mouth to stop myself from crying out.

"My boys are looking after him as we speak," Noah went on. "So, like I said, as usual, I'm a step ahead of you."

The pirate king looked from Noah to Sam. Then he scratched his head. "I'm not sure what you are saying, son," he said. "But I can't help agreeing. If you have indeed found yourself a helper with strong local knowledge then, yes, you are definitely a step ahead."

Sam didn't say anything. He just stared at his brother, his face as red and angry as mine felt.

The pirate king cleared his throat. "OK, let's get down to business," he said. "I am almost ready to retire. You know what that means, don't you, boys?"

"It means I'll finally get what's coming to me," Noah replied, nudging Sam with his elbow. "Lucky me, eh?"

"You shouldn't make assumptions," his dad scolded him. "Inheriting a family business like mine does not come automatically with age. You know as well as I do that pirate rules do not work like that."

No. Pirate rules are "Do what you like and don't care about anyone else."

"I have achieved much in my career. And recently I have heard of a prize that would out-weigh anything I've ever achieved."

"What's that, Father?" Sam asked.

Jakob leaned back in his seat. Stroking his mustache, he breathed in deeply. Then he said, "The Trident's Treasure."

The Trident's Treasure?

I'd never heard of it, but I'd heard of a trident. It was what Neptune—the king of all the seas—always had with him. It was as precious to him as his crown, and it had magical abilities. He used it to create storms or curse people or make the sea do incredible things.

Did the Trident's Treasure have something to do with Neptune?

"The Trident's Treasure? What is that?" Noah asked, echoing the questions racing around my head.

"It is the single most valuable chest of treasure in the oceans," his father replied. "In fact, it is so valuable that its very existence is almost mythical."

"You mean it might not even be real?" Sam asked.

His father stopped rocking back in his chair and banged a fist on the table. "Of *course* it is real!

Would I put this much effort into looking for something that did not exist?"

"N-no, Father. I just——"

"You just questioned me! And you will not do so again. You hear me?"

"Yes, Father. I hear you. I'm sorry."

Michele put a hand on her husband's arm. "Jakob, leave the boy——"

"Do not tell me how to bring up my sons!" he snarled, shaking his wife's hand from his arm.

The four of them looked at one another in silence for a few moments.

"Now, then," the pirate king carried on, his voice light and relaxed again, as if he hadn't just practically burst a blood vessel in front of them all, "I'll continue. I had heard of the Trident's Treasure many times, but until recently, it has always been alluded to as though it were a tale out of a book. Something not real. But now I have reason to believe that it is not only VERY real, but it is also very close to where we are right now."

No one replied. I guess they were probably scared of saying the wrong thing and getting their heads bitten off again.

"So here's what's going to happen," the pirate king continued. "I am going to possess this treasure, and when it is mine, I shall retire and one of you will take over as the pirate king."

"And we . . . ?" Sam prompted his father.

"And *you*," his father replied, smiling as he looked from one son to the other. "*You* are going to find it for me. And the one who does will get half of it."

"Um, forgive me," Noah said, "but with something of this magnitude, why leave it to us?"

The pirate king laughed. "Good question, son. And you'll find out soon enough. But first, your ships. Noah, as you won round one, you get to choose your ship first." He got out of his seat. "Come, make your choice."

The three of them passed close to the edge of the stage as the two boys followed their father to one side of the ship. I stood as still as I possibly could. I didn't breathe, didn't move. I pretended I was a statue and prayed they didn't need to come onto the stage for anything.

"Father, why don't I just take the *Sunbeam*?" Noah asked, pausing on the way to a window. They'd stopped about ten paces away from my hiding place. I thought I was going to be sick with fear.

His father stopped and turned to Noah. "Son, you have disappointed me with that question," he said. "I expected better of a pirate prince."

"I'm sorry. I—"

"No matter. The moment's passed." He turned to Sam. "And what about you? You want to sail to the heart of the pirates' world in a glorified rubber raft as well, do you?"

"No, sir," Sam replied firmly. "I want to sail a ship from your fleet. I want to be a real pirate," he said. He sounded like a little boy pretending to be a grown-up and hoping for his father's approval.

His dad nodded as he patted Sam on the back. "Good lad," he said. Sam's face beamed. It made me feel sad—I wasn't even sure why.

Turning back to Noah, Jakob went on. "When you're in charge, you can do things your way. While I'm still the head of the family business, we do it my way. Clear?"

Noah nodded sulkily as the three of them looked out the window.

"We stick to the traditional ships, the traditional methods, and the traditional values," Jakob was saying. "Study them well and give me your decision in the morning. But first, get some sleep, you two. You won't be getting much over the next couple of days."

The boys were still looking out the window.

"Michele," Jakob called across the room. "Come, let's find the finest cabin and get a good night's rest ourselves." He paced back to the table and held a hand out for his wife. As she stood up and gathered her things together, Jakob called back over his shoulder to his sons. "Five thirty tomorrow morning, we meet here. You will choose your ship and I will give you further instructions. And then the real challenge begins. Round one was just the precursor. The challenge will have two more rounds, and it will take two days. Make sure you are ready."

The sons both nodded to their dad.

As their parents left the room, the two boys stood by the window looking out.

"When I'm pirate king, we'll do away with all those stupid sailing ships," Noah scoffed. He turned to face the room. I ducked back even farther behind the curtain. "We will sail ships like the *Sunbeam*."

"*If*," Sam said. "Not when."

Noah paused for a moment, then he burst out laughing. "Oh, brother, you are so funny," he said, wiping pretend tears from his eyes. "You kill me; you really do."

Sam's face had turned red, but he didn't reply.

Noah walked past the stage as he sauntered back to the table. He picked his jacket off the back of his seat and headed toward the door. Just before he reached it, he stopped and turned around. Sam was still collecting his stuff from the table.

"All right, I'm off to see how my new crewmate is doing," he said. "Sleep well, loser."

Before Sam even had the chance to reply, Noah waved a hand, pulled open the door, and left.

Sam was alone in the room. Or at least, he thought he was. I stood there going over everything I'd heard.

I had no doubt, now, that Noah had Aaron — or one of his men did. What I wasn't so sure of was what to do about it. I'd be no match for them. At least, not on my own.

But maybe I didn't have to tackle him alone . . .

Before I could talk myself out of it, I'd pulled the curtain aside and stepped to the edge of the stage.

Sam spun around. "Who's there?" he barked. Then he saw me. "Oh. You!"

I swallowed hard. My throat was about the width of a centipede.

Come on, Emily. You can do this. You've faced scarier people than the scruffy son of a pirate king.

Sam crossed the room toward me. "What are you doing here?" he asked.

I took a breath. Then, keeping my voice as

calm as I possibly could, I answered.

"I know everything that's going on. I know even more than you do," I said. "And I want to offer you a deal."

Chapter Six

"Tell me about this deal," Sam said.

As he came toward me, my certainty wavered. Maybe this wasn't such a great idea. He was the son of a pirate king, after all. What made me think it was safe to put my idea in his hands? Then again, what other choices did I have?

"Hang on. I'm coming down," I said. Mostly to buy myself a couple more minutes to think through my plan.

Sam sat at a table near the stage, pulled out a chair, and narrowed his eyes at me. "Well?"

"Your brother has captured Aaron," I began, sitting down.

"Who's Aaron?"

"My. . ." Why was I hesitating? "My boyfriend," I said.

"Oh. OK, the boy you were with this evening."

"Yeah, him."

"You think that's who he was talking about earlier?"

"I don't think it is," I said. "I *know* it is."

Sam's eyes were still narrowed. "OK, I believe you," he said. "But why? What does Noah want with your boyfriend?"

"He wants him because of what he knows."

Sam nodded. "Noah said he used to live around here or something."

I bit my lip. "Yeah. At Halflight Castle."

"What?" Leaning forward, Sam looked at me intensely. His blue eyes were like tiny daggers. "He *lived* there? At Halflight Castle?"

I nodded.

"And Noah knew this?"

"Yes. He sat at our table earlier, when we were doing the quiz. Aaron answered a question about it and Noah was really impressed."

"I bet he was," Sam mused. "Yesterday, before we boarded the ship, my dad told us we'd need to understand the local area. He told us the names of a few significant places. Including Halflight Castle."

"And Noah didn't waste any time snatching him and gaining an advantage."

"Exactly. That's my brother for you."

Neither of us spoke for a moment. Sam broke the silence. "You said you wanted to offer me a deal. What is it?"

I paused for a second. Last chance to change my mind.

No. I couldn't leave Aaron to his fate on a pirate ship. I had to go through with this plan.

"Capture me!" I said.

"What? Seriously?"

I nodded. "We both want something," I went on quickly. "I want to find Aaron. You want your dad to respect you more."

"How do you know I—"

"I was here, watching you. I saw it all. How you glowed when he praised you. How you burned with the desire to be as tough as your brother. How you couldn't bear to tell your mom to stop babying you."

Sam folded his arms. "Whatever," he grumbled. "Go on."

"So you capture me. Take me on your ship

as a prisoner. I'll go along with it, pretend you're taking me against my will. You'll look tough, like a pirate should be."

"Like my father wants me to be," Sam muttered. "Like I need to be if I'm going to stand a chance against my brother."

"Exactly. Plus, because Noah has Aaron, capturing me will put you even with him. One prisoner each."

"And what do *you* get out of it?"

I hesitated for a second. Then spoke evenly. "You promise to help me get Aaron back."

"How am I supposed to do that?"

"Win the contest. Then you'll be in charge and you can do whatever you like."

"And if I don't win?"

"Then we come up with another idea. But either way, you promise to help me get Aaron back."

Sam didn't reply for a moment.

Finally, he unfolded his arms, leaned forward, and nodded. "OK," he said. "I'll do it. You've got a deal."

The pirate king had told his sons to meet him back in the ballroom at five thirty. It was just after five, and my plan depended on Sam being the only one there.

I'd had a few hours' rest after Sam and I had finished talking and planning. I hadn't managed to sleep much. My mind was too busy with everything. On the way back to my cabin, I'd slipped a note under Mom's door. Half true and half . . . not quite so true. The true part was that I told her Aaron was in trouble and I had to go help him. The not-quite-true part was that I said I was going to get Dad—and maybe Neptune—to help. If I had told her how I was *really* going about it, she'd never have agreed in a million years.

Anyway, it was too late to think about that. I was here now.

"Emily!" Sam called over to me.

"You're definitely on your own?" I called back.

"Yes. Come on. Quick." He waved me over.

I walked over to meet him in the middle of the room as we'd planned. "You remember what you have to do?" I asked.

"I've gone over it again and again in my head. You're sure it's what you want to do, though?"

I thought about Mom, waking up to a note saying I'd gone. Then I thought about Aaron, captured by pirates and taken prisoner by Sam's horrid older brother.

"Yes," I said. "I'm positive."

"OK, let's get ready. They'll be here any minute."

Sam followed me to the buffet table. It still had food on it. The tablecloth came halfway to the floor.

I crouched down and crawled under the table. Sam pulled down the cloth in front of me. As he bent down, he met my eyes. I grabbed the edge of his vest. "Don't let me down."

He ground his teeth together as he stared into my eyes. "I won't."

A second later, he dropped the tablecloth over me and I retreated under the table.

The door opened and I heard more people come into the room. "Five bags of jewels and money and another three bags full of cell phones, laptops, and anything else we thought we could sell," someone announced. It was the pirate king. I guessed Noah had come in with him. "My crew has served me well."

Five bags full of people's possessions? This man was so awful!

"Now, then, boys, gather around and let me tell you what is going to happen next."

I saw three chairs being pulled out, then three pairs of feet under the nearby table.

Once they were sitting down, Jakob explained their task.

"As you know, your challenge is to find the Trident's Treasure. I've divided the contest into three rounds. Round one was last night, and Noah won that."

Noah made a sneering sound.

The pirate king ignored him. "Round two is to find Crystal Bay," he went on.

"Crystal Bay? I thought that was a place in the bedtime stories Mom read to us when we were little?" Noah broke in. "I bet Sam still reads those stories now," he added with a throaty laugh.

I didn't hear Sam react, but Noah's "Ouch, that's my arm!" indicated that he'd probably hit him.

"Settle down, boys; we have a lot to get through," Jakob went on. "And, yes, you are partly right. Like I said last night, you are going to find a place that is so well hidden many people do think it's a fable, a story, a myth. That place is called Crystal Bay. One of many secret bays around a large and complex island. And at the heart of the island is a hill, with Halfmoon Castle at the top."

"Halfmoon Castle?" Noah interrupted. "The sister castle to Halflight Castle?"

"Well done, son. Yes, it is. Halflight Castle is

legendary enough in its own right. Halfmoon Castle is even more so."

Hearing them mention Halflight Castle—where Aaron had lived most of his life—made my chest tighten.

"Halfmoon Castle is known in the pirate world as the holy grail of destinations," Jakob continued. "It is believed to hold the treasure I told you of last night. But finding it is a treacherous and difficult task."

I could hear a rustle of paper. Then Jakob spoke again. "Ah, here it is," he said. "I shall tell you the truth. I have known of this treasure for many years, but I have never believed it was real. Now I do."

"Why?" Noah asked.

The pirate king replied sharply. "Because now I have this." He cleared his throat and began to read aloud.

> *"At Crystal Bay, the Trident's Treasure waits for*
> *   the most strong and wise.*
> *In all the seas, you'll never find so great or valuable*
> *   a prize.*
> *But only if you're led to it by your fair daughter or*
> *   your son,*
> *Can you then say that it's yours to keep. For life,*
> *   forever, you'll have won."*

76

A poem?

There was a long pause. Sam was first to break it. "So you can only keep the treasure if one of us leads you to it?" he asked.

"So it seems," Jakob admitted. "Hence the contest. Round two is a race to Crystal Bay. Round three is to be the first to find the treasure. I shall follow behind you and track you both. One of you will lead me to the riches that will allow me to retire."

"And that one shares the riches and becomes pirate king?" Noah asked.

"Yes, yes. Of course," his father replied. "Like I said. Now, then, let's get on with it. Noah won round one and has his choice of ship. Noah, which vessel are you choosing?"

"I'll have *Lord Christianos,* please, Father."

Jakob laughed. "I thought you would, seeing as it is nearly twice the size of the other. So, Sam, that means yours is *Morning Star.* Both good ships. Your task is to meet me in Crystal Bay. First one there wins round two. And to help you, I have a clue."

I heard another rustling of paper, then Jakob spoke again. "There is another poem. This one is about the place, about finding it." He cleared his throat. Then he read the poem aloud.

*"Find it with math, with a compass and pen.
Or find it by bribing a hundred wise men.
Use a magical crystal that calls through the blue—
You'll be wrong twenty times; only one way is true."*

"That's it?" Noah asked. "That's supposed to be our guide to finding a near-mythical bay?"

"That's all you're getting," his father replied. "Here you go. One copy each." Then a scraping back of his chair. "Good luck to you both. I know who I'd put my money on, if I ever decided to part with any of it. Which is unlikely!" He burst out laughing, and I saw his feet move as he got up from the table. "You have twenty-four hours, sons. First one there wins round two and opens the way for the others to follow. I'll see you there."

Jakob's feet turned as he started to walk away from the table. The others stood up as well. One pair of feet moved in my direction. I was pretty sure they were Sam's.

Right. Time to give Sam the upper hand. Time to start my campaign to get Aaron back from these disgusting people.

I coughed. Just loud enough so he'd hear me.

Come on, Sam. Now's your chance. You have to capture me. Look good in front of your dad and brother. Do it!

"What was that?" Sam's voice.

"What was what?" his father replied.

"Little bro hearing things," Noah mocked him.

"I heard something. I'm sure of it." Sam came toward me.

This was it.

The cloth was pulled aside. A moment later, I saw Sam's face appear on the other side of it.

"I'm sorry," he whispered at me.

"It's fine. Let's do it," I whispered back.

And then everything changed.

"I *told* you I heard something. Dad, Noah, someone was snooping on us!" Sam reached under the table and grabbed hold of my arm. He pulled me out from under the table. Gripping my arm with one hand, he grabbed my shoulder with the other.

"How dare you spy on us!" he growled at me, his face contorted into a nasty snarl.

Even though I knew he was acting, it still shocked me. I hadn't seen him like this before.

"Who are you working for?" Sam asked. "Who sent you? Who do you think you are to listen in on us like this?"

He was good at pretending to be a fierce pirate. So good that I could barely reply through my nerves. It hit me that even though *Sam* was pretending, I was still standing in a room with his brother and his dad, and neither of *them* needed encouragement when it came to being fierce and unpleasant.

"I was just—I came to get some food," I squeaked. "I hid under the table when I heard you coming."

"Don't lie!" he said. "You were spying! And you won't get away with it! I'll make sure of it."

I glanced across at Noah as his brother spoke. His face was all rage at Sam scoring a point for once.

"I will take her prisoner," Sam said. "Make an example of her."

"Fine. Take her with you and lock her in a cabin till you're out at sea," the pirate king said. "Good work, son; good work."

Sam couldn't keep his face from glowing at receiving such praise from his dad. Even if he did manage to whisper, "I'm really sorry," as he pulled me by the arm and yanked me across the room with him.

The pirate king wagged a finger at his sons. "Boys, it's nearly six a.m. You have less than twenty-four hours now," he said. "See you in Crystal Bay. Remember: first one there wins round two."

And with that, he turned and left the room. My life as a pirate's hostage was about to begin.

Chapter Seven

e made our way to the docking station below the main deck. It was dark and echoey down there. Noah had already stomped ahead of us and disappeared.

Maybe he'd gone to check on Aaron.

A couple of the pirate king's crew were sitting on stools by the opening.

"Sam. Wait." I stopped walking and tugged on Sam's arm.

He turned to me. "What is it?"

"We need to make it look real," I said. "Push me ahead of you. Remember to look tough."

The pirates hadn't seen us yet. They were too busy talking and laughing.

"You're right," Sam said. He took my arm and pushed me ahead of him.

As we approached the pirates, they looked up and stopped chatting.

"I'm Sam. I'm the—er—the pirate king's—" Sam began.

"Yeah, we know who you are," one of them replied gruffly. He nudged a thumb at me. "Who's this?"

"My prisoner. I found her spying on us and my dad said she could come with—"

"Whatever," the guy interrupted. "Over there," he said, waving us toward a tender tied to the dock. "I've got a couple of things to finish off here."

The other guy lazily walked toward the tender and motioned for us to follow him.

"Ah. Yes, I think I recognize—" Sam began.

The guy interrupted him. "Let's go," he said. We clambered aboard and sat on a bench at the front of the little boat as he drove us away from the *Sunbeam* and toward a tall ship that gradually came into sight against the dim dawn sky.

The ship had three masts, with three sets of square sails folded at stages up each one. A rope

82

led from the top of the front mast to the bowsprit sticking out the front of the ship. Three triangular sails lay folded along that. The back half of the ship had a long wooden boom running down the center and a huge round wheel for steering. The ship swayed gently on its mooring, its halyards clinking in the gentle breeze.

Under any other circumstances I would have been excited to take a trip on such a beautiful ship. Excitement, however, was not at the top of my list of feelings.

"We're here," the guy at the back of the boat said as we pulled alongside and he threw a rope across to a cleat on the ship. It was the first thing he'd said the whole trip.

"Thanks," Sam said. "I'm sure I've seen both of you around before. You work for my dad. What's your name?"

The guy looked surprised. "Luke," he said.

Sam reached out to shake his hand. "Thanks, Luke," he said.

Luke stared at Sam. Then, taking a hand off his tiller, he wiped it on his leg and reached out to shake Sam's hand.

Sam nudged a thumb at the ship. "I—er— I guess my crew is waiting on board, is that right?"

Luke stifled a laugh. "Your crew?" He shook his head.

"What?" Sam insisted. "I don't get it."

The guy openly laughed this time.

I could feel Sam tensing up next to me. "What's the joke?"

Luke looked up and met Sam's eyes. "*You* are, pal. You're the joke. And the crew you're waiting for? You're looking at it."

"What? You? You're my crew?"

Luke jabbed a thumb back at the *Sunbeam*. "Me and Dean back there," he said. "Plus another guy and a couple of girls who are on board already." He looked me up and down. "And this one here that you've somehow managed to catch."

"Oh," Sam managed to croak. "Right. OK, then. I thought maybe I'd—"

"Be met with smiles and fawning?" Luke asked.

"No! Not at all. If anything, maybe I'd have more crew than that. And, yeah, to be honest, I thought perhaps you'd be a bit more willing."

"We've been around your dad for years," Luke replied with a shrug. "We know all about you. Let's just say that you're not exactly our first choice either."

Sam stared at Luke. "Right," he said. "OK, I see."

"I'm going back for Dean," Luke went on. "The boarding plank is there," he said, pointing to the side of the ship. "Hal's the chef, so he's the one you want to keep happy. Not that Hal does happy. The girls are probably inside—hopefully making up the cabins and cleaning the place up. Get one of them to show you around. We'll be back soon."

Cleaning the place up? *That* was the role of the girls on a pirate ship? I gritted my teeth.

Luke indicated for us to get off the tender. We clambered across the plank, onto the ship. Sam made half a pretense of shoving me ahead of him.

Once on board, Sam turned back to Luke. "We'll see you—"

Luke had already revved his engine and turned away from the ship.

Whether he was coming back or not was anyone's guess. Whether Sam was going to have a loyal crew working for him—that seemed even more unlikely.

As we made our way across the deck, I couldn't help wondering how on earth Sam was ever going to help me rescue Aaron if he couldn't even command his own crew. And I couldn't stop asking myself questions that turned my insides cold.

What if he couldn't? What if I'd made a terrible mistake?

"Let's try down here." Sam pointed to a steep staircase that led under the deck. We had to turn around and climb down it backward.

I set off down the staircase. Sam followed me. At the bottom, we landed in a room with four tables and bench seats around the sides. The ship's dining room, I guessed. Or *saloon,* to use its proper name.

In front of us was a corridor. Sam pointed ahead. "That way?"

I followed him across the dining room.

The corridor was short, with heavy doors on either side. We opened them as we went along. Each one led to a tiny cabin with a couple of bunk beds inside and the last one opening into a small bathroom. At the end of the corridor, a smaller staircase led down to a lower level.

"Let's go down there," I said.

Sam peered down into the even darker darkness below. "What for?"

"You need to find somewhere to put me if you're going to convince everyone you're holding me captive. It looks dark and dingy. Good place for a prisoner, right?"

Sam let out a sigh. "OK," he said eventually. "Follow me."

We made our way down to the lower deck. There were just two doors in front of us. One was a tiny closet. It had shelves lining the walls on both sides, all crammed with jars and cans and boxes of food. That wouldn't work. The chef would probably be in there several times a day.

Next to it was a sliding door with a latch hooked onto a loop at one end. "Look!" I said. "You could put something through the loop and lock me inside."

"Let me see." Sam pulled the door open and peered inside. I looked over his shoulder into the room. A tiny storeroom. A couple of shelves with toolboxes and books on them. A stool in one corner. A door at the back that led to a toilet. It even had a tiny porthole that half opened.

"This will do," I said. "Leave me here."

Sam shook his head. "I don't know. It doesn't feel right," he said. "It's horrible down here."

"It's *supposed* to be horrible! I'm your prisoner, and you're supposed to be a mean, tough pirate! You have to act the part. It's the only way they'll respect you. Let them all know I'm down here; keep me here for a few hours."

"Long enough to show I'm serious."

"Exactly. You have to go in tough. It's like when we get a new teacher at school. They always start off being mean and showing how much trouble we'll be in if we don't do what they say. Then, once we have gotten the message, they can back off a bit and show their nicer side. That's what you have to do."

Sam nodded. "OK, I get it."

I pushed past him into the room. "Come on. Do it. Leave me here. Shove something through the latch and go. I'll be fine."

Sam nodded. "OK. I'll come and check on you really soon."

He slid the door closed and I heard him fumbling around outside. A moment later, something clanged against the door.

"I found a broom," Sam said from the other side. His voice was muffled by the door between us. "I've put it through the latch. I'll be back soon."

"Good," I replied. "Now, go be the captain of this ship."

Without another word from Sam, I heard him moving away and back up the steps.

I tried the door. It wouldn't open.

A cold snake of fear slithered through me as the reality of my situation sank in.

I was now imprisoned in a tiny room below deck, on a ship that was soon to be boarded by a team of unwilling and unpleasant pirates. Excellent.

I sat on the stool, trying to stay calm while my brain fizzed with questions: *What have you done? What kind of an idiot are you? Why would you literally abandon ship to get locked away in a hot, tiny room on a pirate ship— OF YOUR OWN ACCORD?*

I kept trying to tell my brain to stop. Stop thinking. Stop asking questions. Stop, just *stop.* I was here for Aaron; that was all that mattered.

Every time my brain wouldn't behave and do what I told it to, I forced myself to repeat the same thing, over and over again.

We just have to win the contest. Then Sam will be in charge and he can order Noah to give Aaron back. Sam won't leave me here to fester and die. Everything will be OK.

Maybe if I said it enough times, I might start to believe it.

What was that?

A creaking sound. A tilt. Swaying.

We were on the move.

I let out a breath and tried to calm myself down. No point worrying and wondering. There was no turning back now.

I twirled my hair around my fingers as I paced.

Pace, pace . . . I reached the end of the room and turned around.

Pace, pace . . . I reached the other side of the room.

I stopped pacing. It wasn't helping; it was just reminding me how small my cell was.

And hot.

And airless.

I stood on the stool and stretched up to the porthole. There was a catch on the bottom. I managed to push the bottom half open. The gap was about as wide as my finger. But it was something. I shoved my face as near to it as I could and breathed in the fresh air.

OK, that was better. Everything was fine. Nothing to worry about.

BANG! BANG! BANG!

Someone was at the door.

I jumped down from my stool.

"Um. Who's there?" I called.

The reply was a shuffling sound, as whomever it was pulled the broom out of the loop and fiddled with the catch.

I glanced behind me. Should I hide? *Could* I hide? There was a tiny gap at the end of the bottom shelf. I could crawl into it and pull something over me.

Except, there wasn't time. The door was opening.

Instinctively, I shut my eyes, held my breath, and pressed myself against the wall behind the door.

"Emily?"

Sam!

I came out of the shadows. "Did you seriously knock on the door?"

Sam shrugged. "I was just being polite."

I threw my head back and sighed. "Sam, you're not supposed to be polite. You're supposed to be a pirate! Who in his right mind knocks on the door that he himself locked less than half an hour earlier, when he was imprisoning someone on the ship he is supposed to be captain of?"

Sam did a half grimace, half grin thing that made his eyes sparkle bluer than the sea. "When you put it like that . . ." he said.

I couldn't help smiling as I shook my head, despite my situation. "What are you doing here, anyway?" I asked. "You were supposed to be leaving me for a few hours."

Sam turned away as he bit on a thumbnail. "I just wanted to make sure you were OK," he murmured.

"Sam, why are you really here?"

Sam came in and plonked himself on the stool. "It's awful up there, Emily. They hate me already. They've barely spoken a word to me. They keep making little inside jokes that exclude me. I don't think any of them want to be here. They all wish they were on Noah's ship."

91

"That's what *I'm* here for. To help you get their respect. Somehow, I don't think coming down here to complain to me is the best way of doing that."

Sam made a face at me. "You're beginning to sound like my dad," he mumbled.

"Hey, don't compare me to him!" I replied. "I mean, no offense, but your dad is one of the most horrible people I've ever met."

"No offense?" Sam laughed.

"Sorry. But it's true. And, anyway, that's the whole point. You have to act more like him — and more like Noah. Make the crew think you're tough. I mean, you don't have to be horrible. Just — well, you have to act as if you're in charge."

Sam opened his mouth to reply, but before he spoke, there was a sound outside the cabin. Footsteps, coming closer. "Someone's coming down the steps," he whispered in a panicked voice. "Now what?"

"Here's your chance," I whispered back. "Show them you're the boss. I'm your prisoner, remember!"

"OK — but, just so you know, I'm acting. Like last time. It's not real, OK?"

"Of course. Me too."

He jumped up from the stool and stood in the doorway.

A second later, the footsteps landed with a thump.

"Hey, what are you doing down here?" A girl's voice. That was my cue. Time to get our little drama started.

"Please, let me out!" I cried. "It's not fair, keeping me locked up like this. It's cruel and—and unfeeling, and horrible, and mean."

I hoped my acting skills were convincing.

Sam leaped into his role. "I can't talk now," he said to the girl. "Got to deal with this prisoner." He turned to me. "You'll stay in here for as long as I want you to," he said firmly. "You're my prisoner and you'll come out when I say so, not when you ask. You hear me?"

He was good. He almost had me convinced.

"OK. But, please, don't forget me," I replied. "I could rot and die down here."

"What's going on?" The girl's face appeared around the door. She looked young. Maybe a couple of years older than me. She had a round brown face with dark eyes that narrowed as she stared at me. Her hair was braided, with a couple of black ringlets on her forehead. She had a tattoo on one arm: words in swirly writing; I couldn't see what they said. She wore frayed denim shorts and a T-shirt that was covered in oil, or grime, or something.

"Who are you?" she asked, her eyes wide with surprise.

"I . . ." I began.

"She's my prisoner," Sam broke in. "And she wants to get out, but she can't. Not till I say. Because it's my ship, and she'll come out of there when I say so."

The girl stared at him. So did I. He was taking to his role rather impressively.

"You hear me?" he asked, looking between us, challenging either of us to argue. "I'm the captain and *I'm* in charge."

"I hear you," I replied. "You're the captain."

The girl held her palms out in front of her and took a step back. "Cool. Whatever," she said. "You're the boss."

Sam seemed to stand a bit taller as the girl spoke. "I'll send someone down with some bread and water for you," he said to me. "Till then, you can wait in here and stop complaining."

He reached out to pull the door closed.

"Please don't leave me too long," I said as the door closed in front of me. I was only half acting this time. Sam's performance was so realistic he'd almost convinced me he *was* a tough, mean pirate after all.

"I'll come back for you when I'm good and

94

ready," he said. And with that, he pulled the door closed with a clang. I heard him drop the latch and shove the broom back through the loop.

And I was left in the small, dark room, all on my own once again.

Sam and the girl were still outside the door. I could hear them talking.

"Will she be all right in there?" the girl asked. "It's a small room. She's not going to pass out from lack of oxygen or anything, is she?"

"There's a window. She'll be fine, Ana," Sam replied.

"OK. Whatever you think," the girl said.

"Now, go tell the others I'm holding a meeting in the captain's office in an hour. I need to set out some ground rules."

"Yes, Captain," Ana said. It didn't even sound like she was mocking him. He'd somehow done it. He'd managed to convince her that he was a tough pirate captain and someone who took prisoners without a second thought.

Nice work, Sam. Now, just remember to come back and get me, won't you?

I waited to hear their footsteps moving away. I heard one person go up the ladder. Then a pause.

And then . . .

The door was being unlocked again. A second

95

later, it swung open and Sam was in the doorway, grinning like a kid who'd just woken up on his birthday.

"How was that?" he asked. "Do you think she was convinced?"

"It was kind of amazing," I replied. "Scarily so, actually. Firm and assertive might work just as well, you know! Remember, once they can see that you're not to be messed with, you can start to back off with the mean and horrible."

"Don't worry, I will."

"Hopefully, she'll tell all the others you've captured a prisoner and you'll be halfway there," I said.

"That's the plan. And I've got another plan, too," he said. "I'm going to bring you into the meeting I'm holding."

"What, like as guest of honor?" I joked.

Sam made a face. "I was thinking more as walking proof that I'm in charge and they need to take me seriously. It'll be safe by then anyway."

"Safe?"

Sam shrugged. "We'll be far enough out to sea that there'll be no way you could get back to shore, so there won't be any need to lock you up in a cell down here."

"Mm," I said. "Yeah, good plan." I didn't like how it felt to lie to him—but what were my options? Tell him I was a mermaid who could swim back to shore from anywhere we sailed to?

No way. After the conversation I'd overheard, where he and his family had pretty much said that mermaids were the root of all evil, that was the last thing I'd do.

He was backing out of the room and pulling the door closed. "Just hold on another hour or so," he said. "I'll come back for you, and then you won't have to stay in here."

"OK. Thanks, Sam. Good luck!"

He saluted me in a way that made me smile. And then it made me feel guilty. I was here to get Aaron back, not to make friends with some pirate boy. He wasn't anything to me. He was my route to finding Aaron: nothing more, nothing less.

I made myself as comfortable as I could on my stool and settled into the gentle rocking of the ship, while I waited to see what the next hour would bring.

Chapter Eight

I must have dozed off. Next thing I knew, I was leaping off my stool as I was shaken awake by a clanking sound at the door.

Sam came into the room. He had two of his crew members with him: Ana, the girl from earlier and a boy I didn't recognize. He was tall and lanky with a pale face and long red hair tied back in a ponytail.

"Take her upstairs," Sam said firmly.

The two others shuffled in behind him. "We're setting her free?" the guy asked.

"Look around you, Hal," Sam replied. "There's nothing but miles and miles of sea out there. You think she can escape?" He held Hal's eyes and I watched the power battle take place between them.

Eventually, Hal shrugged. "You're the boss," he said, with just enough of a sneer that I could tell he didn't really mean it.

"You go first," Sam said to me. "Up there. And don't try anything clever."

I felt a flicker of nerves in my stomach. I might have Sam on my side, and this might all be an act for *him,* but I already knew that most of the crew members weren't exactly the kind to welcome me aboard with a smile and a handshake. What if they decided not to listen to Sam anymore? What if there was a mutiny and I ended up *really* taken prisoner—and not by Sam but by these guys?

My brain whirred unpleasantly as I climbed up the steps to the deck.

I reached the top and blinked hard. After being locked in a dark room, the sudden sunlight was blinding. I closed my eyes and rubbed them. When I opened them again and looked around, I couldn't help gasping out loud.

It had been almost pitch-black when we'd boarded the ship. Now it was midmorning and the sun was high in the sky.

All the sails were up, flying above us like enormous wings. The ship was on a tilt, the wind moving through the sails with a low hum. Calm blue sea surrounded us on every side. White frothing waves splashed against the bow of the ship as we sliced through the water. Above us, an unbroken blue sky was like a mirror to the ocean. The ship and nature working together, moving in perfect harmony as we slid through the ocean so smoothly.

It was utterly beautiful.

For just a moment, I kidded myself that I was here simply for the joy of it; I let myself pretend that none of the awful things I knew to be the case were really happening. I allowed a moment for my heart to sing, my eyes to drink in the beauty.

Then Hal grunted, "Come on. Let's get going," as he gave me a nudge — and the spell was broken.

"In here." Sam pointed to a door in the center of the deck. We stepped inside, into an office with bench seats and a table. He nodded to a corner. "Sit over there," he said to me.

I sat where he'd pointed, and we waited as the rest of his crew filed in.

There were six of us here. Ana was on my left.

Luke and Dean were on my right. Hal stood in the corner by the door.

Sam was perched awkwardly on a stool in front of us. He took a breath, then swallowed. "OK, here we all are," he said, his voice shaking.

Out of the corner of my eye, I noticed Luke nudge Dean and laugh. Dean rolled his eyes in reply.

"I mean, obviously not *all,*" Sam went on. "Kat's at the helm." He cleared his throat again and wiped an arm across his forehead.

This was getting worse. Sam caught my eyes as he glanced around the room. His face was bright red. I tried to give him an encouraging look. He gave me a quick nod.

"OK, look, let me start again," he said. "You may not like me. You might not want to be on this ship. I'm guessing at least some of you probably asked for a transfer to my brother's ship when you heard you were with me."

Hal looked down and shuffled his feet. Dean made a loud scoffing noise. Luke stifled a laugh.

"Thought so," Sam said. "But here's the thing. I don't care. I'm not here to make friends, and neither are you. I'm here to do a job, and you're here to help me. This is a contest, and I plan to win it. If you want to be on the losing side then I suggest you do what you like and ignore everything

I say. But if you want to win, we need to be a team. Anyone got a problem with that?" He glared around the room. No one replied.

"Good," he went on. "First off, this is Emily. I captured her on the cruise ship. She has local knowledge that could be helpful in our mission."

Dean slouched forward. "If you captured her, shouldn't she be in a cell or something?" he asked. His voice was rough and gravelly, and he didn't look at me as he spoke.

"We are now twenty miles from land and getting farther away by the minute," Sam replied. "There's no chance she could swim back to land without risking her life."

I squirmed uncomfortably in my seat.

"So I have decided to release her. She's no threat and she's more use to me as crew," Sam went on. "Any more questions?"

No one said anything.

"Good. So let's get to work. We got ourselves out to sea in good time. Now I need to share the challenge with you."

Sam explained the task that he and his brother had been set. We had twenty-four hours — less than that now — to find a bay that was legendary, mainly for the fact that barely anyone had ever found it. We had a crew who looked at best uninterested, and at worst possibly mutinous, and a prisoner who was there under false pretenses.

Oh. And a poem.

"Here's what my dad gave me," Sam said, pulling a piece of paper out of his pocket. "It's a clue."

He unfolded the paper and then read aloud the poem I'd heard Jakob read out to him and Noah on the cruise ship.

"Find it with math, with a compass and pen.
Or find it by bribing a hundred wise men.
Use a magical crystal that calls through the blue—
You'll be wrong twenty times; only one way is true."

The room went silent again.

"That's it?" Ana piped up.

Sam turned to her. "Yes," he said. "That is it. That's all we have to go on."

"That's ridiculous," Dean moaned. "How on earth are we supposed to find somewhere that probably doesn't exist when all we've got to go on is a stupid poem?"

"Good question," Sam replied, ignoring the rude manner of the question and just focusing on the facts. "It's going to be hard. But here's the good thing. Noah has only the same information. At this moment, the stakes are even."

Luke snorted under his breath. Sam ignored him.

"They are as even as they're ever going to be," he went on firmly. "My father is retiring. He's looking for a successor. Whoever wins this contest will be the pirate king." Sam looked around at his reluctant crew. "If I win, I will handpick the most loyal, trustworthy, and capable people to join me, and they will have the best of everything."

He paused. When he spoke again, something had changed. He sounded . . . in charge.

"So come on. Let's get on with it and give it our best shot. Luke, take over from Kat at the helm and send her in here. We'll fill her in on what we're doing, and we'll take turns steering the ship. From this point onward, we have one aim and one aim only: to get to Crystal Bay before Noah. Agreed?"

A few of the crew members mumbled their acknowledgment.

Sam banged his fist on the table. "I said, *Agreed?*" he shouted.

This time, there was a moment's pause, and then everyone replied as if with one voice.

"Agreed!"

We split into groups to work on ideas. I was put with the girls.

"I'm Kat, by the way," Kat said as she squeezed in to join us at the table.

"I'm Emily," I said as I studied her. She was taller than Ana. Her hair was blond and rough like straw, her face ruddy and red from a life on the sea. Like the others, her clothes were simple: shorts and a T-shirt. She had a belt with a big skull-and-crossbones buckle on it.

"Here you go," Sam said as he passed us. He gave us some charts to look at, a couple of pens, a copy of the poem, and some scrap paper.

"Don't worry if you can't figure it out," Dean said as he left. "I'll come and help when I've finished with the sails."

As he walked away, Kat raised her eyebrows so high they disappeared into her hairline. "Did he really just say that?" she asked. "I mean, of course, we're only *girls*. Our brains clearly aren't as good as theirs. *Seriously?*"

Ana burst out laughing. I let a smile play on my lips.

"I think they expect us to just sit around simpering and smiling at them and telling them how mean and cool they are," Ana said.

"I think they've forgotten how we girls got here," Kat replied.

"How *did* you get here?" I asked.

Kat answered first. "My dad's a banker; my mom's a teacher. They sent me on a couple of adventure trips when I was little, and I caught the bug."

"For this?"

"For adventure. For a life on the wild oceans. For something other than growing up in a McMansion like theirs, with a perfect lawn and spotless curtains, saying a polite 'good morning' every day to neighbors I can't stand."

"Why a pirate, though?" I asked.

Kat shrugged again. "Show me another life where a girl can spend the day fixing things, catching fish, climbing ropes, sailing through storms. Show me a world where she can live by her own rules—and maybe I'll consider exchanging this one for it. I had started working on a different ship. One of the guys there always used to antagonize me and tease me. He thought it was fun. I thought it was annoying."

"So what did you do?" I asked.

"I challenged him to a duel," Kat said with a grin.

"You did what? Does that really happen?" I asked. "Like, in real life?"

Kat laughed. "Yep. A dawn fight on the main deck. I got the whole crew to watch. Took me thirty seconds to get him in a headlock on the ground, begging for forgiveness."

I laughed. "I'm guessing he didn't bug you after that?"

"Nope. And word got around about it, so Jakob offered me a job."

"What about you?" I asked Ana. "How did you end up here?"

Ana shrugged. "I grew up in a small town. It was fine when I was little, but when I hit high school, everything fell apart. My parents split up, I got bullied at school, my grades suffered. Fell in with a bad crowd."

"And they led you here?" I asked.

"What? No! The bad crowd was who I came here to get away from!"

"Oh! Sorry," I mumbled.

Ana batted my apology away with her hand. "It's fine. I had a couple of bad years. Got into a few scary situations. Then one day, couple of years ago, a guy I knew said someone was looking for crew. He didn't tell me the guy was a pirate, just that he had a fleet of incredible ships. I went along to apply, and—well—I got hired. Dad was long gone by then, and Mom was just happy I'd found something that I liked, so I joined up."

"What she's not telling you is that they took tests, hard physical tests, and Ana came in at the top," Kat broke in. "As in, top of them all. She beat all the boys."

"Wow. You're both pretty impressive," I mumbled, feeling out of my depth, in more ways than one.

"I don't know about that," Ana said. "I just know that being on a ship like this—it's the only time I feel free."

"Living outside of all society's petty rules and regulations," Kat added. "It's the only way you get to find out who you are, instead of who society wants to mold you into."

I couldn't speak for a moment. Something about their words felt as if it were snaking all the way through me and lighting something up inside me.

"So, what about you?" Ana asked. "How exactly did you end up here?"

I shrugged. I didn't dare tell them too much, not yet. "Vacation gone wrong," I said with a grimace. Before they could ask any more questions, I quickly added, "But I'm glad to have met you girls. I've never really hung out with girls like you before."

Kat laughed. "I'm not sure there *are* many girls like us!"

"Hence why we're not psyched about being told that making sense of a few lines on a piece of paper might be beyond us!" Ana said with a laugh.

I remembered what Luke had said about the girls when we'd come aboard. That they were probably cleaning the cabins and making the beds.

Should I tell them what he'd said? I didn't want to make things worse, but something made me want to tell them. What was it? A desire to fit in? To show them I was like them? Impress them?

Why would I want to do that? Impress a couple of pirate girls?

I knew why.

Because despite the fact that, yes, they were pirates, and, yes, their morals might be a million miles from mine, I couldn't deny that I was a tiny bit in awe of them both already.

It wasn't just the stories of how they'd gotten here. It was the way they looked, the way they carried themselves. So at ease in their bodies, so confident, and so cool with their tattoos, their cutoff denim shorts, strong arms, and grubby faces.

I'd never met girls like them.

In a weird kind of way, I felt that I was like them. I was different from all the girls I'd grown up with my whole life, because I was half mermaid. But I was different from all the mermaid girls, too, because I was half human.

Ana and Kat lived outside the norm, too. And that meant we already had one thing in common, even if I'd never be able to tell them what it was.

So instead, I leaned forward, and in a conspiratorial voice, I said, "Shall I tell you what Luke said when I came aboard?"

The girls both stared at me with identical looks of surprise on their faces. Then Ana shrugged. "Yeah, tell us."

Should I? Was it betraying a teammate? No, it was fine. Telling them was more important than protecting him.

"He, um, he said that you'd probably be inside cleaning the rooms."

The girls stared even harder at me, then looked at each other. Ana shook her head. "See, *that's* what we're up against. They think that they're the only ones who can be pirates. When it comes to climbing up to the crow's nest to fix a broken mast in a force-ten storm, who does it without hesitation?"

"You?" I ventured.

"Dead right. They're all talk. Act tough, talk to us like we're their maids, but somehow do these clever little disappearing acts whenever there's *real* work to be done."

I laughed.

"Remember that time the cables snapped on

the forestay and we had to braid them together with pliers to make them stick?" Kat asked.

"Uh-huh," Ana replied. "Didn't three of them try it?"

"Yep, and three of them failed," Kat said. She held out her arm in a pose like a bodybuilder. "Till I had a try. Then, what do you know? I fixed it."

"If Luke thinks we're here to change his bedsheets and wash his undies, he can flipping well think again," Ana said.

"So let's show them," I said, before I could stop myself. "Let's be the ones to figure out how to get to Crystal Bay. Let's be the best!"

Ana let a slow smile spread across her face as she studied me. "Yeah," she said. "Let's do just that."

Kat grinned and nodded. "You're on."

Ana held her hand up for a high five, first with Kat, then with me. We slapped palms, and then, as we got down to the business of studying the charts and poem, and discussing possible routes and plans, I tried to fight down the warm feeling spreading through me.

I kept telling myself, *They're pirates, they're pirates. They can't be my friends.*

I tried to convince myself that the only reason I wanted to work so hard with them was to stand a better chance of finding Aaron.

But I had to admit to myself that there was more to it than that.

Being with these girls, working together, laughing together, sharing ideas and plans—it was the first time I'd ever felt like I was with girls who were like me. Girls whom I could be myself with.

And I had to admit something else, too.

I liked it.

Chapter Nine

*A*na and Kat were looking at the chart while I studied the poem again.

Find it with math, with a compass and pen.
Or find it by bribing a hundred wise men.
Use a magical crystal that calls through the blue—
You'll be wrong twenty times; only one way is true.

I couldn't make sense of it. All I knew was that Noah had an advantage over us. For one thing, he had Aaron, who would be better than anyone with the math and compass part—*if* Noah could persuade him to help them. And then they had Noah himself, who wouldn't hesitate with the part about bribing a hundred wise men.

And what did *we* have? A reluctant captain, a crew who would mostly rather be anywhere than working for him, and a fake prisoner.

Our chances of winning this thing weren't looking great.

No. I couldn't go there. I shook off my doubts and tried to think. I had a deal to keep, and I needed to stick to my side of it. So I leaned forward and studied the charts with the girls.

Which was when it hit me.

I knew this chart! I'd studied the very same one with Aaron. And I knew something else.

"We need to find Halflight Castle," I said.

"Halflight Castle? Sam told us about that," Kat replied. "It'll be on here, won't it?"

I shook my head "It's kind of a secret. It's not on any charts. It's hard to find—but there should be indicators of some sort. Here, let me look." I traced a circle around a wide area of sea, including the section we were in now. "It's here somewhere. I'm sure of it. Finding it is our first step to finding Halfmoon Castle."

Ana looked at me. Squinting as she stared, she asked, "How do you know?"

I paused. I couldn't exactly tell them that I'd swum there through a long underwater tunnel, and a magical ring that belonged to Neptune had led me there, despite the castle being shrouded in a mist that kept it hidden from most people.

"I, um, well, my boyfriend told me about it," I mumbled.

It seemed this was the right thing to say as they both smiled. "Boyfriend, eh?" Kat asked. "Bit young for a boyfriend, aren't you?"

"I'm thirteen," I said with a shrug. "I mean, he's like my best friend, really. One of them."

"But with kisses?" Kat said, then burst out laughing. Ana grinned.

"Well, yeah, maybe, sometimes," I admitted. My cheeks felt as if they were literally about to burst into flames.

"Come on. Stop teasing her," Ana said, nudging Kat. Then she turned back to me. "So, tell us more."

"About my boyfriend or about Halflight Castle?" I asked.

Ana shrugged. "Both," she said with a grin.

"Well, my boyfriend is named Aaron," I began. "He was on the ship with me."

"The cruise ship that Sam captured you from?" Ana asked, wide-eyed.

"Mm-hm," I replied. I still felt awkward about

the whole pretending-to-be-captured thing, but I had to keep it up. I paused for a moment. Could I tell them the truth? A bit of it at least? I couldn't think of a good reason why not.

"Aaron was captured too," I said. "By Noah."

"What?" Kat burst out. "Seriously?"

"So Sam captured you to get one up on Noah?" Ana asked. "Good for him." She nodded her head appreciatively. *Yes! That part of the plan had worked.*

"Aaron knows this area really well," I said. "I'm fairly sure that's why Noah captured him."

"How does he know it so well?" Kat asked.

"He used to live here."

"He lived here? Like, out here at sea?"

"No." I shook my head. "He lived at Halflight Castle."

The two girls stared at me with identical looks on their faces. Eyes wide, mouths open, speechless.

"He, um, he told me about it," I went on. "It's here somewhere. I know it is. And if Halfmoon is its legendary sister castle, I think finding Halflight Castle is our best first step."

The two girls looked at each other and both gave a slight nod. Then Kat shoved the charts toward me. "I like the plan," she said. "OK, you're in charge. Let's find Halflight Castle."

It was about an hour later and my stomach had started growling with hunger. I hadn't had any breakfast. I assumed the rest of them had eaten while I was locked up. My brain was complaining almost as much as my stomach. We'd been studying the charts and looking out at the sea really hard, and nothing had clicked yet.

"We need fuel," Ana said, shuffling around to the end of the bench and getting up. "I'll go see if Hal needs any help with lunch."

"We'll keep at this," Kat said.

"OK. Back soon."

As she left, I looked back at the chart. I was trying to find something—anything—that I recognized from the time I swam to Halflight Castle.

"What's that blob there?" Kat asked, pointing to a tiny piece of land with danger symbols all around it. It was a really small shape, but from the markings it looked like it was definitely a land mass; it looked like a tiny hill sticking up out of the ocean.

Wait.

The idea of it was familiar. When I'd been to Halflight Castle, our boat had gotten stranded in the middle of the sea. We'd literally washed up on a tiny piece of land and gotten lodged there.

Maybe this was it. I studied the area around it and found something else. A symbol I didn't recognize.

I looked it up in the chart's key. "Bad visibility."

That was it! Halflight Castle was shrouded in mist. You couldn't see it was there most of the time.

"Kat!" I exclaimed. "I think you've got something! I think you've found Halflight Castle!"

By the time Ana got back with some sandwiches, Kat and I had figured out that we were maybe fifty or sixty miles away from Halflight Castle. Kat had estimated that as long as the current wind direction and speed stayed the same, if we kept all our sails out, and all worked around the clock, we could get there by nightfall.

"Let's tell Luke," Kat said. "He's at the helm."

They both got up from the table, leaving their sandwiches half finished.

I cleared my throat. "Wait."

The girls stopped where they were. "What is it?" Kat asked.

"We should tell Sam, not Luke," I said quietly. "Sam's the captain."

Kat made a scoffing sound. "Whatever," she said.

"What is it?" I asked. "What have you got against him?"

Kat shrugged. "We haven't got anything against him," she said. "He's just . . ."

"He just hasn't got what it takes," Ana finished. "No offense. He's an OK guy. Just not cut out to be in charge. He doesn't fit the mold."

"Come on," I said. "Listen to yourselves. Doesn't fit the mold? Surely you've had people say the same about you. How many girls go around with a penknife tucked into their belt and a wrench in their pocket at all times?"

Neither of them replied.

"How many girls braid each other's hair and fasten it with ship's wire instead of pink ribbons? How many girls can fix a cable on a forestay?"

"That might be true," Kat conceded. "But so what? What's your point?"

"My point is that you're making up your minds about him without giving him a chance."

I watched the girls' faces as they considered what I was saying. I realized I was holding my breath and I couldn't figure out why. Then Ana replied.

"Emily's right," she said. "Maybe we could give him a chance."

"OK, fine, whatever," Kat said. "We'll give him

the benefit of the doubt—for now. I'll go talk to him, see what he wants to do."

"And in the meantime, I'll have a word with Luke anyway, see if he can alter his course slightly while we—I mean, while Sam—figures out the next step," Ana added. "How does that sound?"

They both looked at me and I realized they were waiting for a reply. How did I get to be in charge all of a sudden? I was supposed to be the prisoner!

"It sounds sw—" I began. I nearly said it sounded swishy. *Swishy* was a mermaid word. "It sounds great," I said with a smile. "I'll stay here and study the charts a bit more, see if I can find anything else on them that might help."

"OK, let's go." Kat headed for the doorway.

Ana stopped her. "Wait," she said. Then she paused. She scratched her neck and looked at the floor.

"What?" Kat asked. "What is it?"

"Just . . . maybe one of us should stay here," she mumbled eventually.

"Emily's staying here!" Kat replied. Then she looked at me. "Oh," she said. "You mean . . ."

She didn't finish her sentence. She didn't have to. "I'm not going anywhere," I said. Nudging a thumb at the doorway—at the ocean surrounding us on every side—I added, "I couldn't get anywhere anyway, could I?"

"No. Sorry. OK," Ana said. "I mean, I don't want to treat you like you're—"

"It's fine," I said with the biggest and most understanding smile I could muster. "I understand. But you have my word. I'm not going anywhere."

The girls left to do their jobs and I sat at the desk, trying to do mine. Which I might have stood at least a tiny chance of doing if it weren't for the fact that my brain kept going over their words again and again.

I would *never* be accepted by them. They would never see me as one of them.

And for the first time in ages, I couldn't help wondering if I would ever *really* fit in anywhere.

Chapter Ten

*E*veryone was hard at work.

Ana and Luke were planning the route. Sam was at the helm. Kat and Dean were working the sails. Hal was lookout. And I was helping out wherever I could, mostly pulling on ropes and keeping the deck clear and tidy.

There was just one problem.

We weren't getting anywhere.

As we sailed, the sky grew murky. A mist started to settle around us.

We shifted jobs as we sailed through it. I was put on watch with Ana and Dean, all three of us looking out for anything we could spot in the mist that was settling more and more heavily with every passing minute.

Every now and then, we'd think we'd seen something, but it would turn out to be a bird. A couple of times, we saw something bigger in the distance. We figured it was Noah, floundering around in the mist nearby.

At least that meant he hadn't found it either.

The more we sailed on, the more hopeless everyone started to feel. Dean was getting grumpy. Even grumpier than before.

"What's the point of this?" he grumbled. "We're never going to find it. We might as well give up."

"Don't say things like that," Ana replied. "You should know better than to talk about giving up."

"Why are we following Sam's orders, anyway?" he went on, ignoring what Ana said. "The guy clearly doesn't know what he's doing. He's driving us into the thickest fog I've ever seen in my life. What kind of a fool *is* he?"

"He's not a fool," I began. "He's just trying to—"

"I'm not planning to die out here. You hear me?" Dean carried on as if I weren't even there.

"If it comes to it, if he expects us to go down with the ship, I'm out. Or he is. We should all get together, take over, knock some sense into the guy." He swung on one of the halyards, punching his hand into a fist as he leaned forward into the wind. "Come on. Let's do it!"

"Dean, stop it!" Ana scolded him. She was half laughing. I guessed she was assuming he was joking. I hoped she was right.

"Stop what?"

I spun around. Sam was behind us. He must have handed over the helm to one of the others.

Dean let go of the halyard and jumped back down onto the deck.

No one replied.

"I said, *Stop what?*" Sam repeated. He was trying to sound firm, but his voice had a wobble to it.

Dean opened his mouth to reply.

"We were just messing around," I said quickly, before Dean could say anything. "Weren't we, Dean?"

Dean looked at me as if I were a fly that had fallen in his dinner and then turned into a giant beetle in front of his eyes. I didn't care. I stayed calm and stared back at him.

Eventually, he lifted a shoulder in a lazy shrug. "Yeah. We were just messing around," he repeated.

"Fine. Well, I'm glad that's settled," Sam said tightly. "And I'm glad you're getting along and having fun. I'd hate to think anyone was having mutinous thoughts. I really would prefer not to have to discipline anyone at this early stage."

He looked pointedly at Dean as he talked. He clearly knew Dean had said worse than we'd told him, but he was letting it go for now.

"OK," Dean said. "I get it."

Sam slapped him on the back. "Good." Turning around, he called over his shoulder, "Another half hour and we'll switch the shifts. Let's get ourselves out of this fog."

As Sam disappeared out of sight, Dean turned to me. "Why'd you do that?" he asked.

I decided to reply in the kind of language he'd understand. With a shrug.

"But really," Ana added. "Why did you? You could have turned Dean in right then if you'd wanted to."

I sighed. "Because we're a team. Maybe we should start acting like it. It's the only way we'll get out of this."

Neither of them replied for a moment. Finally, Dean gave me a sharp nod. "All right," he said. "Whatever. I'll give it a try. For now."

"Yeah, me too," Ana added. "Let's cut the guy some slack — and let's just get back to work."

I couldn't help smiling. "Great," I said, maybe a bit too cheerily. They might have agreed to give Sam a chance, but they were still pirates locked in a battle out at sea, not happy campers on their way to a vacation.

At least we had a plan. It was better than the near mutiny we'd had five minutes earlier. And for now, I'd consider that to be a win.

Looking out from the deck, I stared into the thick mist. It was so heavy now that I could barely see beyond the ship itself. We were still just about making progress through it, white frothing waves splashing against the bow as we sailed on blue, blue water.

We had to find a way out of here. But how? The air was so thick with mist we could be turning in circles and we wouldn't even know it.

Wait.

The air. The *air* was thick with mist.

What about the sea? Maybe I could see farther if I was underwater.

The thought pulled at me. As it did, I remembered a line from the poem.

Use a magical crystal that calls through the blue.

Maybe there was something down there, in the blue; something magical. Something that could help us.

And maybe I could find it.

I looked around. Everyone was busy with their jobs.

I crept to the very front of the ship. The bowsprit bounced almost to the edge of the water as we sliced through the waves.

One last glance behind me. Still no one around. OK. This was it.

I took one more step to the very edge of the ship, clambering onto the gunwales. A final glance around.

Now!

I jumped.

The moment I hit the water, I flipped myself over and zoomed straight down.

As I swam deeper, I felt my body start to change. My legs stiffened and tingled as they began to join together. Soon, they had completely disappeared. In their place, my tail had formed.

I was a mermaid again.

I allowed myself a minute to enjoy the feeling.

It was like breaking out of a prison and experiencing freedom after years in a cell. It was like feeling the sun on my face after the longest winter. It was like coming back to myself after being lost for longer than I could bear.

As I let the feelings of joy wash over me, a thought came with them.

I could escape.

I could swim away. They'd never find me, especially in this mist. They'd never know what had happened to me. I'd never have to see Sam's face turn to disgust and horror when he found out I was a mermaid. I wouldn't have to suffer the inevitable consequences when we lost out to Noah and became his servants, or prisoners, or whatever he decided to do with us.

I could go home to my family and pretend none of this had happened.

Apart from one thing.

I was here to find Aaron—and I couldn't do any of those things knowing that he was still being held prisoner on a pirate ship.

No. My only option was to keep trying to help Sam win the race and then make sure he came good on his promise to free Aaron.

I swam back up toward the surface to get my bearings. The ship had already sailed farther into the mist. I swam toward it, to keep it in my sight.

I didn't want to lose them altogether. That would ruin everything.

Once I was close enough to follow the ship's trail through the water, I dived down again.

I was right. It was clear. I could see ten times farther than above the water. I looked around. I barely even knew what I was looking for—but I kept one phrase in my mind. One line:

Use a magical crystal that calls through the blue.

And I made a silent promise. If the magical crystal was here, I would find it.

A sleek black fish with big white eyes slithered by without a second glance. A large shoal of tiny black fish came close to me, buzzing like a spinning top as they moved together in perfect synchronicity, their shape barely altering as they spun through the water.

Below me, the ocean floor seemed a long way away. Rocks, reeds, darkness. I suddenly felt very alone. A shiver ran through me, from the top of my head to the tip of my tail.

Shaking off my anxiety, I swam on. And on.

There was nothing down here. Nothing magical. Just dark, wide ocean—and me.

What exactly was I doing here?

What had I been thinking? I always thought I could save the day, didn't I? One day I'd learn that I couldn't do it every time. Maybe one day I'd learn to stop chasing after trouble.

Maybe.

But not today. Because a moment later, I saw something out of the corner of my eye. Something bright and sparkly. It looked silver. It looked like crystals glinting against the current.

Had I found it? The magical crystal?

Making a quick mental note of exactly where the ship was, I turned and swam as fast as I could toward the silver flashes. I couldn't wait to tell them I'd found it. Everyone would be so happy. The girls would be proud. I'd be —

I reached the magical crystal. It wasn't a crystal at all. And it wasn't magical. It was a large silver fish, shooting out sparkly darts of light across the water as it slithered along.

I swam back toward the *Morning Star,* feeling more hopeless than ever.

And then I felt it.

A current.

At first, I thought it was from the ship, pulling me along in its wake. But I wasn't directly behind the ship, so it couldn't be that.

What was it, then?

Something came into my mind. The other time I'd felt this. It was when I came to Halflight Castle for the first time. I'd been wearing Neptune's ring and it had led me through the water, pulling me along in a current that felt just like this.

Could this be . . . ?

I didn't dare hope. Instead, I simply let the current take me. With the slightest flick of my tail, I zoomed along, following its path. Soon, I'd overtaken the ship. I could see the hull behind me, getting farther away.

What should I do? Each time I looked back, the ship was more distant. If I got too far away, I might never find my way back. But I couldn't resist the current. As it pulled me along, the sea grew clearer and clearer. It was so blue I felt almost as if I were flying through the clearest sky.

And then . . .

What was that?

A sound. A gentle tinkling. Almost like a birdcall, or a delicate bell. I bent my tail to try to create at least a bit of resistance against the tide. It worked. I was slowing down. I glanced behind me. The ship was still in sight. Good.

Now, what was that sound? I ducked down and tried to dive. It was tough. The current was still pulling me forward but I managed to inch gradually down.

Soon, I'd reached the ocean floor. I skittered across it without even trying, gliding so quickly across the seabed that the sand below me exploded in great blinding puffballs. The tinkling sound was getting louder. It was as if it were calling me—and the current was leading me to its call.

My heart thudded fast.

Use a magical crystal that calls through the blue.

This was definitely calling. And until the sand had started billowing out like this, the water had been the bluest I'd ever seen.

I swam on. The sandy floor gave way to rocks. I whizzed across the top of hermit crabs hanging out in front of their caves. I held my stomach in as I flickered close to a rock covered in sea anemones. I marveled at the fish darting around through rocky channels: blue, orange, spotted ones; others with large red mouths.

And then I saw it.

A huge jagged rock, standing upright like an obelisk. Hooked over the top was a silver chain. Looped onto the chain: a crystal. It looked like a mini version of the glitter ball that they hung on the ceiling of the gym for school dances.

The blue water, the glittering crystal. The tinkling sound that had called me over. This had to be it! It *had* to be.

I swam over to the rock, diving down to take a closer look. As I reached out for the chain, I could see it was stuck between two rocks. Pushing hard against the smaller one, I gradually inched it out. Then I lifted the chain over the top of the obelisk-shaped rock and held the crystal in my hand.

It had so many sides—each one flashing a silvery reflection of my surroundings.

Wait. What was the last line of the poem?

You'll be wrong twenty times; only one way is true.

Did the crystal have twenty sides? Was it showing me twenty different reflections?

My head was full of questions—but I didn't have time to dwell on them, or count the crystal's edges. I had to swim back up to the surface. In the time I'd been down here, I'd lost track of the ship, and if I hung around any longer, I'd be stuck out here in the middle of the ocean on my own.

I carefully placed the silver chain around my neck, then I flipped myself upward, kicked my tail, and swam back up to the surface.

I couldn't wait to get back to the ship and show the others what I'd found.

Chapter Eleven

I broke through the surface of the water and looked around.

The thick mist still surrounded me, but it had risen a tiny bit. There was a gap between the bottom of the mist and the ocean's surface — just wide enough for me to peer through. I slowly spun in a circle, scanning what I could see of the horizon through the gap.

There! The ship was some way off, but I could see the hull, slipping along through the mist.

I threw myself into a dive and swam hard to catch up with the ship. Soon, I was back in its wake. Nearly there.

I paused as I kept pace with it. What was I going to say to Sam? How could I explain what I'd found? Make something up? I didn't want to lie to him. Tell him the truth? I couldn't take that risk.

I shook off my questions. I would worry about it when the time came. For now, I had to figure out how to get back on the *Morning Star* and transform into my human self without being seen.

I surfaced as close to the ship as I dared. I could see a couple of people on the back deck, looking all around. I ducked back down, flicked my tail like crazy, and swam to the front of the ship.

I resurfaced and trod water with my tail as I wiped my hair out of my eyes. Perfect. There was no one around. This was my chance.

I spun my tail as hard as I could, to get momentum to dive out of the water. Then . . .

Jump!

I splashed back down before I could reach the deck. The ship was bouncing on the waves so hard I'd have to time it perfectly.

I watched, counted, waited, and then . . .

Go!

I leaped right out of the sea and grabbed a

chain that was looped around a ledge on the bow. I pulled myself out of the water and perched on the ledge, watching my tail flap against the hull as I caught my breath. After a while, I felt the familiar feeling of my tail disappearing. Soon, it had gone completely, and my legs reappeared.

Holding on to the chain with one hand, I rubbed my legs with the other to bring them back to life. Once the numbness, and then the pins and needles, had gone, I pulled myself to my feet and, crouching low, looked across the deck.

Clear.

As I straightened my legs, I remembered the crystal. I felt for the chain around my neck. Yes, still there. I pulled it off and held the crystal in my hand. It made me feel calm, somehow.

After putting it in my pocket for safekeeping, I climbed over the ropes lying coiled on the deck and made my way toward the center of the ship deck. I could see Sam and Kat standing near the wheel.

They looked up as I approached. I held my breath. Had they noticed I'd disappeared? Was this going to be the end of the good feeling and being welcome on the ship? Was I about to get thrown back into the cell on the lower deck?

There was only one way to find out.

"Hi." I approached Sam and Kat, hand in pocket, casual tone in my voice.

Sam looked up and grinned. "Hey, Emily. I was wondering where you were."

"Just around," I replied, hoping neither of them would notice my cheeks burning up. I've never been any good at lying.

"You're drenched," Kat said.

"Oh. Yeah, I — I, um, got splashed by a wave."

Kat nodded. "It's rough, isn't it?"

"See anything useful out there?" Sam asked.

I paused before answering. "Umm," I mumbled.

"I don't know what we're going to do," Sam jumped in before I could figure out what I was going to say next. "We're going in circles. Every time I think we're making progress, we pass a mark that we'd passed an hour earlier and I realize we're not getting *anywhere*."

"Mm," I said again. Helpful.

I waited till I could see that Kat was concentrating on looking ahead, then I motioned for Sam to come closer. "Can I talk to you for a minute?" I asked.

"Sure," he replied. "What's up?"

"In private?" I whispered.

Kat glanced at us. Then she gave me a knowing wink. What, exactly, she meant, I wasn't sure. "Don't mind me," she said. "Go have your little private chat. I'm fine here."

Sam nudged a thumb toward a bench halfway up the ship. "Let's go sit down," he said.

I followed him along the deck and we sat on the bench together.

Sam turned to me. "So, what's up?" he asked.

"I . . ." I began. I didn't know how to continue. I needed to show him what I'd found. If there was even the slightest chance it could help, I *had* to. But I couldn't tell him how I'd found it. I hated the fact that I couldn't tell him, hated how it made me feel. But I wasn't prepared to take the risk; not yet, anyway.

"Are you OK? Are you sick?" Sam asked. He pushed his hair out of his eyes. I noticed his hands were hard and red. Life on a ship did that to all of them. As I chewed on a finger, I realized it was starting to do it to me, too. And I liked it. Weird. Dry, chapped hands. Why on earth was that something I wanted?

I shook my head. "Nothing like that."

"What, then?"

I took a breath and slowly let it out. "I've found

something. If I show you what it is, you have to promise me you won't ask how I found it."

"But—"

"But nothing. That's the deal. You don't need to know how I got it. All you need to know is that I've found something I think might help us."

Sam shrugged. "OK," he agreed. "I promise."

I paused.

"What?" Sam asked.

I thought for a moment. There was still something I needed to know about Sam before handing over the best clue we had. Still something I needed to be sure about. "Why do you want to win so badly?" I asked. "This ship, this life. Being a pirate prince. Growing up to be like your dad. Is that what you want? I mean, *really* what you want?"

Sam's eyes flashed. "Yes," he said. "And no."

I folded my arms. "Go on."

He turned away from me. "No, of course I don't want to be like my dad. But—well, he's still my dad. Is it so wrong to want him to be proud of me?"

Before I could reply, Sam continued on. "Is it so awful to want to see my mom look at me without pity, or my brother look at me without sneering? Is it really so terrible to want their approval and respect?"

I thought about Sam's words for a while. "I don't think it's terrible to *want* it," I said carefully. "But why do you *need* it?"

Shaking his hair off his face, Sam spoke to the wind. "Because without it, what have I got? If I'm not part of this family, I don't know who I am."

A couple of strands of hair fell back across his face as he turned back to me. His eyes were the color of the sky as they held mine. "You have no idea what it's like," he said. "Spending all your life trying to be what others want. Trying so hard to please them and make them happy that you lose sight of what makes *you* happy."

I thought about how hard I'd found it to decide which way to go home. How I was so worried about offending Shona or upsetting Aaron. I thought about how much I wanted to keep Mom happy and make Dad proud of me. I thought about how I couldn't admit to being a mermaid because I knew Sam and his crew would find me disgusting. And if *they* thought I was disgusting, I might start to believe it myself.

"Yeah," I said softly. "I do know what that's like, actually."

Sam stared back at me. He was looking at me so intensely I felt as though he might see inside my head. "Really?" he asked. "How come?"

I shook my head. "Just take my word for it," I

said. "I understand better than you'll ever know. And I know you're sick of how your family treats you. But there's still one thing I *don't* get. Still one thing you haven't answered."

"What's that?"

"How far are you willing to go to get their respect? How much do you want it? Enough to be a pirate just like them? To be as cold and unfeeling as they are? If it means finally taking your place in the family, is that what you want? To live your life like they live theirs?"

Sam looked away as he chewed on a fingernail. Not that there was much nail left to chew on. Finally he turned back to me. "No," he said. "That isn't what I want. But I don't know anything else. This is my life. It's the life I've been born into and I don't know any other."

"You could fight it," I suggested. "Or run away. Leave them to it."

"Ha!" Sam shook his head as he laughed bitterly.

"What?"

"Run away? I'd never outwit them. I can't escape my family. They'd catch me in no time — and the punishment would be harsher than I care to think about."

"So, then, do the opposite," I said.

"What's that?"

"Make sure you win. Like we've agreed. If you get to make the rules, you don't have to do what *anyone* says."

"That's the plan," Sam said. "And you're right. If I win——"

"*When* you win," I corrected him.

Sam smiled. "OK, *when* I win, I promise we'll do things differently."

His words had convinced me. "OK. In that case, let's make it happen. We can do it," I said.

Sam grinned.

"What?"

"You said 'we.' You're in this with me? Not just to help Aaron but actually for *me*?"

"I . . ." I mumbled. I hadn't even realized what I'd said. Was he right? *Did* I want to help him for his reasons? Why on earth should I care about what happened to a pirate family? All I cared about was why I'd come here in the first place.

Wasn't it?

"Look, I want you to win," I said quickly. "That should be enough. You do it for your reasons; I'll do it for mine."

"OK. Whatever you say," Sam said with another smile. When he smiled like that, I could let myself forget where we were for half a second. I could strip away the expectations, the contests, the traitors and thieves, and just pretend we were a normal boy and girl, just hanging out on a daytrip on the ocean.

And then almost immediately, I hated myself for thinking that.

"Now, are you going to tell me the thing you wanted to tell me?" Sam asked before I got too lost in confused thoughts.

"On one condition."

"What's that?"

"That whatever happens, you stop trying to be what you think everyone else wants you to be, and you just be you."

Sam looked at me for a long time, his face suddenly serious. Then he said, "I will if you will."

Still holding my eyes, he held out a hand.

I took his hand and shook it. "OK," I said. "You've got a deal."

Sam let out a breath and sat back. "So, what's the big, important thing you have to tell me?"

"It's not something I have to *tell* you," I said. "It's something I have to *show* you."

I reached into my pocket and pulled out the crystal. I held it out toward him.

Sam leaned forward. "What is it?" he asked. He took it from me and examined it. The crystal flashed reflections of the water in every direction.

"I think it has about twenty sides," I said. "I haven't counted them yet, but there are lots."

"Twenty sides?" Sam asked. "So what?" He studied the crystal for a moment. "I mean, it's pretty, but I don't get why this is so important."

I waited a beat before replying. I wanted him to figure it out for himself. He turned the crystal over in his hands.

There! I saw it! One tiny flash of something other than ocean.

You'll be wrong twenty times; only one way is true.

I couldn't wait any longer. "Sam," I said urgently. "It's the crystal from the poem."

I watched the facts click into place in Sam's eyes. "Wait—you mean, my dad's poem?" Handing me back the crystal, he rummaged in his jeans pocket.

He pulled out a torn piece of paper, unfolded it, and read aloud. *"Find it with math, with a compass and pen. Or find it by bribing a hundred wise men. Use a magical crystal that calls through the blue. You'll be wrong twenty times; only one way is true."*

Sam folded the paper back up. His eyes were dancing with life. "Emily," he breathed. "You found it. You found the crystal! I don't know how. I don't care." He jumped up from the bench and pulled me up with him. "We're going to win!" he said. "We're going to beat my brother!"

Grabbing hold of me, he pulled me into a hug. I paused for a moment, then I hugged him back.

Sam pulled away and took my hand. "Come on," he said, grinning. "Let's tell the rest of the team."

As Sam called everyone together, I tried not to think about the fact that Sam had hugged me. I tried not to dwell on how good it felt to be part of the team. I tried not to think about any of it. All that mattered was winning this contest.

For everyone's sake, including Aaron's.

Chapter Twelve

The mist still hadn't lifted—but our moods had. Everyone agreed that finding the crystal was the first break we'd had.

We passed it around so that each of us had the chance to give it a really good look.

"Where did you say you found it, again?" Dean asked, giving me a sideways glance as he took his turn examining the crystal.

"Emily spotted it in the netting on the bow-sprit," Sam answered quickly, before I had a chance to reply. "We must have picked it up on some of those rough waves back there."

"Is that right?" Dean asked, still looking at me.

"Yeah," I said quickly. I turned away and started fiddling with a rope so he couldn't see my face — and cursed myself once again for being so bad at lying.

Why had Sam covered for me? Did he know how I'd *really* found it? Surely not. He couldn't. There was no way I'd still be on board this ship if he knew I was a mermaid.

I batted away that thought and shook off the accompanying discomfort before it took root.

"Come on," Ana said. "It's the middle of the afternoon. We're almost halfway through our time. We need to figure out how to use it."

"Ana's right," Luke added. "Just because we've found a tool that *might* help us, doesn't mean we've won this round of the contest yet."

I stepped forward and held my hand out to Dean. "Can I . . . ?" I asked. He handed it to me.

"I've been looking at how it works," I said. "It shows reflections from all of its sides. But every now and then, there's a flash of something different."

"Like in the poem," Kat said.

I turned to smile at her. "Exactly. And I've noticed something else, as well. It seems to show a brighter image than we can see with our eyes. Look." I held the crystal up in the air. "Do you see?"

The others crowded around. "It's showing the ocean where we can only see the mist!" Ana exclaimed. "That's amazing. It's . . ."

"Magical!" I finished. "So I'm thinking, we should position it somewhere high up while we sail. If it's got the ability to burn through the mist, then maybe it will show Halflight Castle before we can see it with our eyes."

"Sounds like a long shot," Dean muttered.

"Have you got a better idea?" Sam asked.

Dean replied with a shrug.

"In that case, here's what we're going to do," Sam went on. "We're going to put it at the top of the mast and see what happens." He looked around at us. "We'll each take turns doing an hour's watch from the crow's nest. Kat, you can go first."

Kat nodded. "Will do."

Sam turned to Ana. "Ana, you're on chart work. Keep an eye on our position in relation to the maps."

Ana nodded. "OK."

"Luke, you're on the helm. Dean, you're in charge of sails. Shout if you need anyone to help you."

Luke and Dean both did a kind of shrug-nod back at Sam.

"Hal, you're on food. And can you draw up a schedule for all this?"

"Sure," Hal replied.

Sam turned to me. "Emily, you're on lookout from the deck."

"No problem," I said.

"I'll keep an overview of everything and will cover for anyone who needs a break or an extra pair of hands." Sam looked around at everyone again. "We're all clear on what we have to do. Any questions?"

No one said anything. I felt as if they could also see what I was seeing—and hearing: Sam was starting to sound more confident, more in charge. More like a pirate prince.

"All right, come on; let's go!" Sam shouted. "Let's get to work—let's win this contest!"

As the meeting broke up and we all got started on our tasks, I could feel the change in the air. We were finally starting to work as a team. And for the first time since I'd come on board, I found myself starting to believe we might even stand a chance of being the *winning* team.

We were on the third shift change and hadn't had a breakthrough yet. The jubilation of only a couple of hours ago was already starting to give way to feelings of hopelessness and failure.

I waited for Ana to come down the mast. It was my turn next. I watched her climb down with the ease of a monkey shimmying down a tree. I knew she'd been doing this for years, like the rest of them, but I still envied her bravery. I hadn't told anyone, but I was a bit nervous about going all the way up the mast for my shift.

"Don't worry, you'll be fine," Ana said, glancing at my face as she jumped the last section to land on the deck next to me. She unclipped two hooks and handed me the harness. "Put this on."

I pulled it tight and buckled it around my waist. "Just stay hooked on at all times and you can't fall more than the length of your arm," she said as she checked all the buckles.

I held my arm out. OK, that wasn't too bad. I could do this.

Ana patted my back. "Ready?"

"Mmm-hmm," I said. And then, heart beating like the wings of a butterfly trapped in a jar, I looked for my first foothold.

The first few steps weren't too bad. I reached as high as I could, gripped the sides of the rope ladder, and stepped up the first rung. I reached up again, hooking the safety clip onto the side, and took another step.

"You're doing great!" Ana called up to me. "Just take it slowly."

"OK!" I called back, without looking down. Step by step, rung by rung, clip by clip, I inched gradually up until I'd reached the platform.

"You did it!" Ana called.

I looked down to give her a thumbs-up. Whoa! Big mistake. I hadn't realized how far up I'd climbed! Ana looked like a little toy person. The deck was a long way away. The sea was even farther. And I was up here, rocking wildly from side to side as the ship swayed through the ocean's swell.

Each time the mast swayed sideways, my stomach felt as if it had been left on the opposite side.

I gripped the mast and tried not to think about it.

I'm fine. I'm clipped on. I'm safe.

I kept repeating those words to myself like a mantra. After a while, my heart rate calmed down and I started to relax. I settled into my position and got to work. I had a job to do.

The crystal's chain was looped over a hook on the mast. It swung a bit with the ship's motion, but I could see it clearly enough. Not that there was much to see. Just reflections of the sea, with a thin line of mist slicing through the middle of each one.

I kept watching. Sea and mist. Nothing but sea and mist.

Had I gotten it wrong? For the first time, I doubted myself. Why had I been so convinced this was the magical crystal? Why did everyone believe me so readily? Was it just that we wanted so much for it to be true—and we didn't have anything better to go on?

What if we were *all* wrong? What if we'd wasted two hours on a wild-goose chase while Noah powered ahead and won the contest? What then?

No. I couldn't let myself go down that road. We *had* to be right.

I stared at the crystal so hard my eyes began to water. Wiping my hand across my eyes, I whispered to it.

"Please show us the way. Please be the magical crystal."

And then . . .

I saw it.

Just a glimpse. Something other than blue sea and white mist flickered out from the crystal. Something that looked like . . .

There it was again! And I knew exactly what it was.

A hill. A tiny piece of land. A building on top of it.

Halflight Castle. We'd found it!

Almost as soon as I saw the image, it disappeared. I gripped the mast more tightly, stared at the crystal more intently, and willed it to appear again.

And then it did; only, this time, it wasn't just one image. This time, the mist cleared from the reflections and the castle appeared in them all!

"Ana!" I called. She was still on the deck below me.

She glanced up. "You OK?" she asked.

"Get Sam. Tell the others. I can see Halflight Castle in the crystal!"

"Are you kidding me?"

"I'm serious!" I called. "We're on track. We're nearly there!"

"Which direction?" Ana called up to me.

I studied the crystal again. How could I tell? The castle was reflected in every side. It could be anywhere.

"I don't know," I said honestly. "But it's nearby. I'm sure of it."

"OK, stay there. I'll get Sam." Ana turned and made her way to the back of the ship. I continued watching the crystal. It was like looking through one of those kaleidoscopes I'd had when I was little. Like I was seeing hundreds of pictures of the same thing, turned into tiny patterns that were mesmerizing me.

Except—there was something still not right about it. I couldn't think what it was. Then I thought about the poem again.

You'll be wrong twenty times; only one way is true.

We weren't supposed to be following twenty versions of the same picture. We were supposed to be following the one that was *different* from all the others. So even if we managed to figure out which direction the picture of Halflight Castle was pointing to, that wouldn't give us the answer we were looking for.

I was pondering all this when Sam appeared below me. "I'm coming up!" he called.

Bounding up the ladder as expertly as Ana had come down it, he was by my side a minute later.

"Ana says you've found the castle," he said.

I frowned. "Yeah, but it's not the right one."

"Not the right one?" Sam pointed out to sea. "All we can see with our bare eyes is ocean and mist. If the crystal is showing a castle, surely it has to be the magical one we're looking for."

"I don't know."

"Let me have a look. Swap places with me."

Sam shuffled around the platform and I

squeezed myself against the mast to let him get past me. He leaned over to look at the crystal.

"Wow," he breathed. "That's amazing." He turned away to look around the ship. "It's showing us something that isn't even there."

"Yeah, Halflight Castle is a bit like that," I admitted. "But the poem said the picture would be wrong twenty times, and we have to look for the one that is right."

Sam frowned. "Maybe the poem was wrong. Maybe the crystal is telling us the right thing twenty times over!"

"But it's not telling us anything—it's pointing in *every* direction!" I said.

"Hmm, I see what you mean," Sam agreed.

We stood there together, watching it for a while. It was mesmerizing, watching the crystal sway gently, flashing and flickering with multiple pictures of the same thing. Except . . .

"Sam!" I grabbed his arm. "Look!" I'd seen something different. So subtle you wouldn't have noticed unless you were searching for it.

Sam continued looking at the crystal. "What is it?" he asked. "What have you seen?"

"Keep watching."

We stared together. "There!" I jabbed a finger at the crystal. "Do you see it?"

155

"What am I looking at?" Sam asked. "I can't see anything different. Just twenty tiny pictures of a castle."

"Keep watching. I've counted the sides. There are twenty-one, but when the sun catches it, one side looks different from the others. It's so tiny you could miss it if you blink, but I'm sure it's—"

"There it is!" Sam burst out. "I saw it! I saw it! I saw something different."

As we watched, we managed to pinpoint the side that was different. It was to the left of the ship—the port side. It was hard to see it most of the time, but every now and then the sun glinted sharply against the crystal, and we could tell that this one picture was different. All the others showed a castle with a line of mist running through the middle. This one looked identical, but instead of a line of mist, the castle had a chunky crescent moon above it.

"Almost half a moon," I murmured without thinking about it.

Sam turned to me. "Halfmoon Castle—that's what we're looking for. The picture has a moon in it!" He let go of the mast and threw his arms around me. "You did it, Emily—you found it!"

I couldn't reply for a moment. Sam's grip had taken my breath away. He let go of me and stood back, grinning. "We're going to beat Noah. I know it," he said. "Thanks to you."

Finally, I found my voice. "It's a team effort," I said.

"Well, OK. But I'm glad you're on my team."

"Me too," I said before I could stop myself.

Sam had pulled a compass out of his pocket. "Looks easterly to me. I'm going to take a precise bearing, then let's go down and tell the others. We'll keep taking turns up here, checking the crystal to make sure we maintain the right direction. And we'll work around the clock till we get there."

"Sounds like a plan," I said.

"Come on. Let's go tell the others."

"I thought we had to keep someone up here all the time," I said.

"Come down with me first. I want you by my side when I tell everyone what you've found. You deserve your moment of glory! It's Luke's turn on watch next, so he can take over once we've shared the good news."

I was glad Sam climbed down the mast ahead of me. I was blushing furiously from his praise and I didn't want him to see it.

Daylight was starting to fade. The sun was halfway down from its spot in the sky, burning through the mist as it headed for the horizon behind us.

"You're sure this is right?" Dean asked. "Seems to me like we're just going deeper and deeper into that fog."

Sam was at the wheel, with Dean and me on either side of him, keeping watch. Not that there was much to see. To be fair, Dean was right. We could still barely see a thing. We'd been following the crystal for a couple of hours now, and, if anything, the mist was even thicker than it had been earlier.

"Shall I check with Kat?" I asked. It was her turn on watch.

"I'm sure we're on the right course," Sam replied. "She'd have called down if not."

Dean grumbled something under his breath.

Sam turned to him. "You got something to say, Dean?" he asked sharply.

Dean put his hands in his pockets and shrugged.

Sam stepped to the side. "Emily, take the helm for a minute, will you?"

I moved into his place at the wheel. "I haven't done it yet," I said nervously.

"You've sailed a boat before, though, haven't you?"

"Well, yes, but —"

"Just hold the wheel; keep us on the same bearing."

I nodded and took hold of the wheel. "OK."

I watched Dean and Sam square up to each other out of the corner of my eye.

"If you have something to say, I'd rather you say it," Sam said to Dean.

"Yeah, I'm sure you would," Dean replied.

"What's that supposed to mean?"

Dean took his hands out of his pockets and waved them at the ship. "This!" he said. "All of it. We're in a contest out at sea, in the middle of the thickest fog in the world, and what are we doing about it? We're listening to some mumbo jumbo about a piece of jewelry that's supposedly magical; we've got girls running the show; and we've got you wanting to *talk* about it." Dean hissed through his teeth. "It's embarrassing," he added.

"Embarrassing?" Sam replied. "What's embarrassing about it?"

"You're supposed to be a pirate. I'm supposed to call you *Captain,*" Dean replied. "Neither word fits you. I'm ashamed to be on the same ship as you."

"Oh, really?" Sam replied. "Well, if you feel that strongly about it, I'm sure we can find ways to solve that problem for you." He waved a hand at the plank of wood we'd used to get across to the

159

ship when we'd boarded. "Go ahead; you're free to leave anytime you like."

"Ha! You want me to walk the plank?" Dean scoffed. "That's your solution? Even when you *do* act like a pirate, it's more like one from a corny old movie than a real-life, modern-day pirate. It's bad enough that your dad is a caricature of a pirate but you're just as bad. The only one in your family with any idea of modern pirating is your brother. And believe me, if I get half a chance to jump ship, his is the one I'll be joining."

Dean's voice was rising with each word. Others were starting to notice. Ana poked her head out from inside the office. Luke was making his way across the deck from the front.

"Everything OK here?" Luke asked as he joined us.

"It's about as OK as it will ever be with a clueless, hopeless loser in charge, clutching at straws and hoping for magical jewels to solve our problems," Dean replied.

Sam's face was bright red. He looked like he was ready to throw Dean off the ship himself, never mind make him walk the plank.

Ana had joined us too. "What's up?" she asked. "Anything I can help with?"

"I think we're beyond help," Dean mumbled.

"Dean, come on," Luke said.

"Come on, what?" Dean snapped back. "You know you agree with me."

"I . . ." Luke began.

"Dudes, what's going on?" Hal had come over to join us.

"Nothing much," Ana replied. "Just the usual arguments."

Hal started to ask something else. I didn't hear what he said, as Dean and Sam had both raised their voices and Luke was shouting louder than them both to try to tell them to stop arguing. Soon, everyone was talking—and *no one* was listening.

Everything was falling apart. How had it happened so quickly? A couple of hours ago, we'd been a team, ready to steam ahead and win round two of the contest. Now we were nothing more than an arguing crowd.

I held the wheel tightly and focused on the figures of the dial in front of me. I had one job: keep us on course. Even if that course was starting to seem pointless. Even if it was beginning to seem like we'd barely last another five minutes without having an outright mutiny on our hands.

And then I heard a voice. Someone was calling.

"Hey," I said. No one responded. They were too busy yelling at one another to notice me.

161

Again. The voice. It was Kat! She was shouting from the top of the mast and waving down to us.

"Guys!" I said more firmly.

Still no reply.

"Hey!" I yelled. "Just shut up and listen, will you?"

That did it. All of them stopped talking and turned to look at me.

I pointed above us. "It's Kat," I said. "She's calling us."

Everyone looked up. She was waving madly at us with one hand; the other holding tightly on to the mast.

"What is it, Kat?" Sam called up to her.

"We're there!" she called back. "The crystal's leading us there."

"Seriously?" Ana stepped forward and shouted up. "It's working?"

Kat grinned widely. It changed her whole face, took the hardness out of her features. "It's working!" she said. "I can see land ahead."

I turned to Sam. His eyes were wide. "You're sure?" he called up.

"Absolutely positive. It's a huge bay, looks like golden sand and turquoise water."

"Crystal Bay," I breathed. "We've found it."

Dean hadn't said anything yet. Sam turned to face him. Squaring up to him so that their faces were almost touching, he said, "Want to call me a loser again, Dean?"

Dean stared Sam in the face, but Sam didn't back down. Eventually, Dean shrugged. "Whatever," he mumbled.

He turned away from Sam and was about to walk off. "Hey!" I called to him.

Dean turned to me. So did Sam. Sam flashed me a *"What are you doing?"* look. I didn't care. I'd promised Sam I would help him get the respect of his crew. I had to do this.

"Sam knows what he's doing," I said, my heart thumping with nerves as I spoke. Why would Dean listen to *me*? "He's the captain. It's time you recognized that."

Dean's eyes opened so wide his eyebrows practically disappeared into his hairline. "Says who?" he asked with a sneer. "The onboard prisoner who's only been let out of her cell while we're too far out at sea for her to run away?"

Half of me wanted to reply by telling him how wrong he was. That, actually, I could leave anytime I wanted. The other half of me knew that announcing I was a mermaid to the whole crew would be the *worst* thing I could do right now.

Either way, I didn't have time to reply. Sam did it for me.

"Actually, no. That's not who she is," he said.

163

With a glance at me, he added, "At least, it isn't anymore."

"What do you mean?" Luke asked. "If she's not a prisoner, what is she?"

Sam took a breath, pausing before he replied. Then he said, "She's the person who just found the most important thing we've managed to come up with since we set foot on this ship. She's the person who might have just saved all of us from humiliation and defeat." He turned to me and smiled. "She's the person I am officially declaring one of the crew."

"You've got to be kidding me," Dean murmured under his breath.

"That's the end of the discussion," Sam said, taking charge again. "We've got more important matters on our hands. Like winning round two."

Before anyone had a chance to argue with him, he went on. "Luke, can you take the helm? Stay on this course unless we say otherwise."

Luke nodded and came to take over for me.

"Emily, I want you to stay between the mast and the wheel. Listen to Kat's instructions and pass them straight on to Luke. We need every move to be accurate now."

"OK," I replied, and started picking my way across the deck.

"Ana and Dean, I want you both on the sails. Dean, you're in charge on the deck. You are the most skilled at trimming the sails with fine precision."

"How did you—?" Dean began.

"I watch. I observe," Sam cut in. "I'm the captain. It's my job to notice these things."

For once, too stunned to argue, Dean simply nodded.

"If either Dean or Kat say we need to make an adjustment, I want it done instantly," Sam carried on as Dean made his way to the sails. "Come on, now, crew. Our goal is in sight. Let's put aside personal feelings and win this thing."

As we got to work, I could almost feel the air change around me. It started with Sam. It was as though he'd suddenly developed a belief that he could do it—not just win this round but be the captain of the ship. And his belief was infectious—at least, to most of us. Dean would probably never respect Sam or his instructions, but at least he'd stopped arguing. Even *he* knew it made sense to work together now.

I stood on the deck, listening for instructions from Kat, passing them on to Luke. I felt like a cog in a machine that was working smoothly and efficiently. I was part of the machine, part of the crew. I had a weird feeling that I was with my people.

My people? A bunch of pirates?

The feeling didn't make any sense, so I shrugged it off and got on with my job.

Chapter Thirteen

I'd arrived on beautiful beaches before now. I'd sailed to incredible places, swum with the most enchanting animals, been greeted by sights that had taken my breath away. But I had never experienced the feeling that washed over me as we sailed into Crystal Bay.

If you added up the thrills you got for every birthday and each Christmas morning, you might get close.

And not just because of how beautiful it was: the sea was so clear we could see the seabed;

hundreds of multicolored fish, coral-covered rocks, and dancing reeds lay below us when we were still half a mile out. They were as clear as if we were looking at them through polished glass.

Ahead, the sand looked as soft as fine sugar and was the color of the purest gold. The sunlight sparkled on the waves like tiny crystals.

Hence the name, I guessed.

It was completely beautiful. But that wasn't the reason I felt so good. At least, not all of it.

It was also the fact that we were the only ship in the bay. Which meant we'd done it. We'd gotten here first.

We dropped anchor in the bay and started pulling down the sails.

Sam was walking around with the biggest grin on his face. "Crew meeting, guys," he called. "Finish what you're doing and meet me at the wheel in five minutes."

I pulled on the mainsail's ropes with Ana. Once the sail was down, I watched how she neatly looped her rope, then did the same with mine.

"Nice work. You're a quick learner," she said as we walked over to join the others.

"OK, gather 'round," Sam said once we'd all arrived. Most of us sat down, but Dean stood, holding on to the barrier at the edge of the deck. Sam was standing next to the wheel.

All the sails were down. Other than bobbing gently on the light swell in the bay, the ship was still and silent.

Sam couldn't keep the smile off his face. "Well done, crew," he said. "We did it. We got here first. We beat Noah!"

"Well done, Captain!" Kat said.

"And Emily," Ana added.

Luke stepped forward. "You did a good job," he said to Sam. "Nice one."

Dean shuffled his feet. "I thought we were a team?" he muttered.

"We *are* a team," Sam replied.

"So we should be saying 'Well done' to all of us, not just *Captain Sam* and his freshly promoted prisoner." He loaded the "Captain Sam" with heavy sarcasm in his voice.

"Chill out, Dean," Kat said. "Can't you give him a break for two minutes?"

Dean shrugged and looked at his watch. "All right. Two minutes," he said.

"You can say what you like, Dean, and you can be as miserable as you want, but you're not going to change the fact that we—yes, *we*—have just scored an amazing victory," Sam said. "And I, for one, am not going to let anything, or anyone, spoil it."

Hal was looking out to sea. "Sam," he said without turning around.

"What?"

Hal pointed to where he was looking. "I think we've got company."

I couldn't see what he was pointing at. Now that we were in Crystal Bay, the mist had mostly cleared up, but it was still hazy out on the horizon.

Then I saw it: two ships.

"Noah," Sam breathed. "And it looks like my dad's ship is behind him."

"He said the first ship would open the way for the others," I reminded him. "We somehow let them in and they've followed, like he said they would."

We watched the two ships come toward us. Soon they were close enough that we could see the crew on them both.

As they sailed into the bay, Sam breathed out through his teeth. "Here we go," he said. "The moment of truth."

All three ships were moored in the bay. While his crew set about bringing down sails and securing his ship, Jakob came out and stood at the bow. He waved across to us and to Noah.

"Gather your crews and meet on deck in

ten minutes," he bellowed across the bay. "I will announce the winner of round two and tell you what comes next."

Something flipped inside me. If Noah was bringing all his crew members on deck, would that include Aaron? Or would he be locked up somewhere below, like a *real* prisoner should be?

"Announce the winner?" Sam grumbled as I helped him coil a rope on the deck. "Isn't it obvious? *I'm* the winner. I hope Noah isn't going to try to convince Dad that he got here before me!"

"He couldn't do that, could he?" I said. "They both arrived just now; they'd have seen us here. Nothing can stop you from having won this round, surely."

Sam looked persuaded by my argument. It was true; anyone could see that. Still, I had the feeling Noah wasn't used to coming second to his younger brother, and he wasn't likely to take it lying down.

"You both did well," Jakob called to us once we'd all gathered on the ships' decks. The vessels were virtually stepping distance away from one another now, so he didn't have to shout too loud. "Not by much," he went on, "but Sam had the edge." He strode over to the side of the deck closest to our ship. "Sam, you are the winner of round two!"

The pirate king's announcement was met with an instant cheer from our crew. Sam punched the air. Even Dean managed half a smile.

"We did it!" Sam said, turning to give us all a huge grin. "Well done, team."

"That's a point apiece," the pirate king continued once he'd given us a couple of minutes to celebrate.

I looked across at the *Lord Christianos*. Noah was strutting up and down, pointing at his crew, shouting at them. They all stood there, not moving, not responding while he yelled.

"You're a useless bunch of lazy good-for-nothing layabouts!" I heard him shout. "Pathetic. You call yourselves pirates? And you let that waste of space of a brother of mine beat me? I'd throw every last one of you off the ship if I didn't think you'd come crawling back, like the miserable sea rats you are!"

Sam turned to talk to us. Looking mainly at Dean and Luke, he stuck a thumb out at his brother's ship. "Is that how you want me to be? That's how a real pirate captain acts, is it?" he asked. "Still want to join my brother's ship?"

Luke stared openmouthed at the spectacle, along with the rest of us. Dean shrugged and looked at his feet.

"He's horrible," Ana murmured.

Noah's tirade was still going. "I'm disgusted with you! Every last one of you." Marching up and down the deck, Noah paused in front of one of his crew members. I couldn't see who it was, as Noah was standing in the way. "Well, almost every single one," he went on. "*You* are the exception. You and your knowledge saved the day. Come here. Stand beside me."

Noah moved aside and pulled his best crew member forward. I couldn't help gasping out loud when I saw who it was.

"You are my new first mate," Noah announced.

His perfect crew member, the one he'd just promoted . . .

It was Aaron.

From where I was standing, I could practically look into Aaron's eyes as he stood next to his boss. Or I could have, if he were looking my way. He was too busy grinning at Noah.

Sam turned to me. His face was white. "Emily, isn't that—?"

I shook my head sharply. "Don't say anything."

Sam nodded like he understood. But he didn't. He had no idea what I was feeling. The confusion, the betrayal, the hurt. How could Aaron look so happy on that ship? How could he be smiling up at Noah like that? Had he suddenly become loyal to a *pirate*?

But, then, from the outside, wasn't that exactly what I'd done?

In my mind, Sam was different — but maybe Aaron saw something that made him feel the same about Noah?

There *had* to be an explanation for Aaron's behavior. I knew him. He was the reason I was out here! He wouldn't abandon everything he believed in for the sake of a bit of praise from a pirate.

Would he?

Noah strode to the bow of his ship. "A point apiece, is it, Father?" he called. "You *really* have me even with my useless brother?"

"Now, Noah, it's my contest, and your brother won round two fair and square," his dad replied.

"How about some bonus points, then?" Noah called across to him. He held on to a halyard and leaned right out of the boat. "What if I have something that shows how brave and tough and talented I am?" he asked. "What if I prove — as usual — that anything my brother does, I can do better? Would we still be a point apiece then, Father?"

"Son, what are you talking about?" Jakob yelled.

"Wait." Noah swung back onto the deck and went over to a couple of his crew members. I couldn't hear what he said to them, but they both nodded and instantly headed for the stern.

"Give me two minutes and I'll show you," Noah called.

The pirate king pulled a huge gold watch from a pocket on his chest. "You have two minutes, son. Then I will make the result official."

"Official?" Sam blurted out. "What do you mean, *then* you'll make it official? It's official now, isn't it? Round two was to get here first. I got here first. I win! What more is there to it?"

"Calm down, Sam," his dad bellowed. "This is *my* contest, *my* rules. You *have* won round two. But if I decide Noah gains a bonus point, then that is up to me. You hear me?"

"I hear you," Sam grumbled. For two minutes, no one said anything else. The wind softly whistled through the masts and lanyards as the ships bobbed on the gentle waves.

A door opened on the pirate king's ship.

"What's going on, Jakob?" It was Michele.

"Help my wife!" the pirate king barked at his men. Two of them instantly ran over to the door Michele was heaving herself through and held their arms out for her.

She joined her husband on the deck.

"Noah has a surprise for us, my dear," Jakob said loud enough that the wind carried his voice across to us. "He says it will be better than Sam's win."

Michele looked across at us. Beaming, she called to her younger son. "You won! I'm so proud of you, darling!"

Just then, Noah's men came back into view. They were hauling something around from the back deck, something over the side. In the water? "We need a hand here," one of them called over his shoulder to the rest of the crew. "We've got a wriggler."

A wriggler? What did he have? A shark? A small whale? What could he possibly think would earn him bonus points with his dad?

Whatever it was, the men were now hauling it along the side of the deck and starting to pull it up.

A cage. A heavily barred cage.

And inside it, wriggling, fighting, screaming in rage as the cage came out of the water, was Shona.

Chapter Fourteen

or a moment, no one spoke. It was as if someone had come along and switched the scene to mute.

Noah grinned as he paused his strutting up and down the deck. Jakob looked on with an expression that could have been horror—and from what he'd previously said about mermaids, *should* have been horror—but looked more like fascination.

Sam stood with his mouth open, not saying anything.

Aaron had turned away and wasn't even looking at Shona.

And I — what could I say? What could I feel? All I could do was stare at Shona. She had stopped writhing and was staring straight back at me; her eyes were scared black holes.

My feet felt as though they had been bolted to the deck. I couldn't move, couldn't speak. What should I do? If I called out to her, I'd give myself up and could jeopardize everything. If I ignored her, I was turning my back on my best friend. Indecision meant I did nothing, which felt more of a shameful betrayal than any of my options.

Michele was the first out of us all to find her voice.

"What is the meaning of this, Noah?" she wailed, clutching the side rails of the ship as she leaned across to peer at Shona. "First your brother taunts me with mermaid jewelry; now an actual *mermaid*?" Her legs began to give way.

Jakob caught her in his arms and helped her to a bench, where she sat down. She pulled a fan out of her bag and wafted it in front of her face.

Jakob returned to the bow of his ship. He still hadn't said anything. No one had except Michele. It seemed we were all holding our breath, each of us for different reasons.

"Son," Jakob said. His voice was gravel. "What is the meaning of this? Have you lost your mind? Or are you simply intent on upsetting your mother?"

"Neither, Father," Noah replied. "This is a gift, for you."

"A gift for me? A *mermaid*?" Jakob looked as if he were about to explode. "Son, you had better explain yourself, and fast."

"Other ships have figureheads carved out of wood. We sail with them on our bows, to ward off evil spirits and warn others of our intent." Noah spoke quickly. "*You* can have a real, live mermaid—something no other pirate possesses. Keep it alive by putting it low enough that it dips in the water. When you have a mermaid as a prisoner, even your enemies will have to acknowledge that you really are the bravest, the toughest, and the most fearless pirate on the seas."

For a full minute, no one spoke. Noah ran a hand through his hair as he stared at his dad. Jakob looked down at the deck and rubbed his chin, pulling on his beard. The rest of us looked between the two of them, as if we were watching a tennis match. The wind whistled a low, humming tune through sails and lanyards and ropes.

Finally, Jakob turned to his wife. She gave him a curt nod. Jakob turned to Noah.

"Do it," the pirate king said.

Noah punched the air. "Thank you, Father," he said. "You won't regret it."

"I had better not," Jakob replied darkly. He waved a hand at Shona. "You've done well, boy. You've done very well."

"I get the bonus point?" Noah asked.

His dad nodded. "You do. Which now puts you at two points and Sam at one."

"What? That's so unfair!" Sam burst out.

Noah grinned widely. "Suck it up, little bro," he said. "Might as well give up now. You'll never act like a pirate. You'll never even think like one!"

I could feel Sam's rage coming off him. "Seriously, Father?" he shouted. "You're going to let this happen?"

Jakob shrugged, as if it were out of his control. As if it weren't his stupid contest and his stupid rules and him constantly moving the goalposts. "Unless you've got something better . . ." he said.

Noah had instructed his men to haul Shona's cage onto the deck. Shona lay inside it on the floor, barely moving.

"She needs to be in water," I hissed under my breath.

Sam turned to me. "What's that?"

I opened my mouth to say it again—but

nothing came out. I had to protect myself, I had to protect what I was doing here.

But did I? I was here to rescue Aaron. Aaron, who was right now laughing and joking with Noah's crew. It didn't look like he needed me. Even if he did, right now Shona needed me more.

"She needs to be in water," I said again. "She won't survive."

"Who needs . . . ?" Sam began. Then he looked across at Noah's ship. "Oh. I get you. Stay here," he instructed me. "OK?"

I nodded and he marched to the edge of the deck. "Hey!" he yelled. "If you want to hand that thing over to Dad to prove how fearless and clever you are, you'll probably need to keep it alive!"

As he called across, Aaron stopped talking with the guys he'd been joking and laughing with. He glanced at Shona, and, even from here, I could see that his face had turned white.

"Get it back in the water!" Sam yelled.

It.

Get it back in the water.

Sam's words stuck in my throat. I felt as if I might be sick.

Aaron was already rushing over to Shona in her cage. He was beckoning others to join him. I stood mute as I watched them lower her cage, holding my breath till she was back in the water

181

and safe again. As safe as she could be, given the circumstances.

Jakob called across to Noah. "Keep it for now until I decide what to do with it."

Noah gave his dad a salute. "Will do, Father."

"Right. We'll take a couple of hours' break before we head off. Free time, everyone," Jakob announced.

Every word they uttered made me feel worse. The way they talked about Shona. Like she was a thing, not a person.

I had to get away. Had to think. "I'm just going to . . . get something," I said to Sam. I couldn't even make up a good excuse. I didn't care about making excuses — I just needed to be gone.

"What?" Sam swiveled around. "Emily, are you OK?"

"I'll be back in a sec," I said. Then I turned and hurried away from them all, looking down at my feet so no one would see the tears that were already beginning to prick at my eyes.

I sat on a steel box at the stern of the ship, my head in my hands as I tried to figure out what to do next.

The others were all still at the bow. It was safe to let myself register my true feelings for a moment.

But what *were* my true feelings? I almost felt numb. Confused about Aaron, horrified by Sam, disgusted by Noah, furious at Jakob. Yes, all of those. But stronger than any of them was the heartbreak that seared through my body each time I pictured Shona in that cage.

And here I was, sitting crying on a box, unable to do *anything* to help her.

I couldn't bear it.

"Emily?"

I swiped an arm across my wet face and looked up. Sam.

"What do you want?" I snapped.

He sat down beside me. "I wanted to see if you're all right," he said softly.

"What do you think?" I mumbled. "Do I *look* all right?"

Sam didn't reply for a while. We sat together, the sun now beating down on our backs, the water gurgling below us as it swirled around the rudder. The breeze whistled through the folded sails.

"It's all done now," Sam said eventually.

"What's all done?"

"The mermaid. It's back in water."

"Yeah. I saw."

I looked at him. There was something in his voice, something about the way he was talking to me. Like he was trying to tell me something, but without the actual words. What was it?

Who cared? He was a pirate, like his horrible family. Whatever he said, he was just like the rest of them. He'd been brought up to hate mermaids.

It.

"I can't stay here," I said.

"You want to go below deck?"

I shook my head. "On the ship," I said.

As soon as I said the words, I realized how much I meant them. I'd never said anything I'd meant more. I couldn't spend another minute in the company of these people. I could never tell Sam the truth about what I was, and that meant that everything about being here was a lie. If Sam knew what I was, once he'd gotten over the disgust, he'd just trade me to get one over on his brother and even up in their contest.

But it wasn't just that. Being around all this unspoken hatred and disgust was almost making me feel ashamed of *myself.* Like I was something disgusting. I couldn't let them do that to me.

I stood up. "I need to leave."

Sam got up and stood in front of me. "You can't go," he said, his voice raw, almost a whisper.

"Why not?" I challenged him.

Sam waited till I looked at him before replying. "It's not safe," he said.

"What do you mean? What's not safe?"

"For . . ." His face reddened. "For you," he said eventually.

"For me? Because I'm your prisoner?" I blurted out, anger making me braver. "I don't care about that anymore. I have more to worry about than my own safety. Don't you get that? No. Of course you don't get it. You don't get anything. You don't know anything about me, and you never will."

I turned and started to walk away.

Sam grabbed my arm. "Stop!" he said.

I wheeled around to face him. My face right up close to his, I hissed my reply through my teeth. "Make me. Hold me prisoner again. Put me back in that room. Act like a real pirate. Like the pirate you really are. Just like them."

"Emily," Sam hissed back. "Listen to me. I'm *not* like them, and I *don't* want to hold you prisoner. I want to protect you."

"Protect me?" I laughed in his face. My anger making me braver—or more stupid—by the moment, I added, "You wouldn't say that if you knew who I really was."

"That's what I'm trying to tell you!" Sam said. "I *do* know. I know exactly who you are! That's why I want to protect you."

185

"What do you know?" I asked. I stopped breathing while I waited for his reply.

Sam let go of my arm. He held my eyes. Neither of us moved, looked away, or even blinked. "I know," he said, his voice a whisper barely louder than the breeze. "I saw you."

"You saw me? When?" I managed to squeeze the words out through a throat that felt about as thin as a sand eel.

"When you came back on the ship with the crystal. I saw . . . your tail. I know you're a mermaid."

I couldn't speak. *He knew.* He knew all along. He'd been biding his time, and now was his chance. He could throw me in a cage like Shona and be even with his brother. It was all over. I looked down at the floor.

Sam touched my chin, lifted it back up. "Emily, listen to me," he said.

I looked into his eyes. I could feel my mouth start to wobble.

Don't cry. Don't you dare cry.

"I don't care," he said.

I frowned. "I don't believe you."

"I promise you," he said. "It doesn't change a thing."

"It changes *everything*," I mumbled. "You *hate* mermaids. Your family hates them. We're evil;

186

we're bad luck—we're something to capture to show others how tough you are."

"Emily, stop it! Mermaids are none of those things. I've never liked hearing my family talk about mermaids in that way. I've just put up with it and acted as though I felt the same way. But I don't."

I stared into his eyes, trying to find the lie he was telling me. I couldn't see one.

"And no matter what, I could *never* see you as evil or bad luck, or anything horrible like that."

"Why not?" I whispered.

Sam smiled. As he did, I felt my anger start to crumble, my fear start to subside, my outside layer open up to him.

"Because it's you," he said simply.

I couldn't speak. I could barely look at him. His words were melting me. His eyes were boring into me. I felt exposed and confused.

Sam's hand was still touching my face. "You believe me, don't you?" he said. He moved a step closer. There was barely any space between us now.

"I . . ."

"We're the same, you and I," he went on.

"The same?" Even despite everything, I laughed. "How on earth do you figure that?"

"Always busy trying to do what others want us to do. Knowing we're different from how

187

others see us, but always afraid to show who we really are."

I stared at him. "But who I am . . . is a mermaid," I whispered.

Sam smiled again. "Who you are is *you*," he replied. "And you're amazing."

I laughed, mainly to hide my embarrassment. I shook my head, and he let his hand fall back down to his side.

"It's true," he went on. "You and I, we're a team, and teammates look after each other."

"Shona's my team, too," I said, biting my lip as I watched his face.

"Shona?" he asked. "Who's—oh. The . . . mermaid?"

I nodded. I could feel my eyes sting again. "She's my best friend," I managed to squeeze out.

Sam exhaled. "OK," he said carefully.

"So, if you really understand me as well as you think you do, then you'll know what I have to do."

"Yeah," he said. "I think I do."

I moved to turn away from him. "And if you understand, you won't try to stop me."

"Emily, wait!"

"I have to save her, Sam. I can't just stand by."

"I know. I know. But—look. If you go now, they'll catch you too. Everyone's out on deck;

everyone's looking. What use will you be to your friend if you just get thrown in a cage with her?"

"I . . ."

"We need to do this carefully, think it through. We need to make a plan."

"We?"

"Emily, when are you going to get it? We're in this together. You and I. You've helped me. And now I'm going to help you. That's how it works."

"Even though I'm a mermaid?" I asked.

Sam laughed. "*Especially* because you're a mermaid. Emily, you've already helped me realize about a hundred ways that I don't want to be like the rest of my family. Their . . . mer-phobia? That's just another one."

Sam sat down on the box and patted the space next to him. "Now, are you going to join me in figuring out how to rescue your friend, or am I going to have to figure it out on my own?"

I couldn't speak for a moment. My throat was clogged up with emotion. Instead, I sat down beside him, and together, we began to form a plan.

Chapter Fifteen

*I*t was an hour later and I was ready to go.

Noah's ship had moved farther out into the bay. We'd watched the crew gloating as they sailed away: striding around, punching the air with their fists, partying, and throwing trash overboard.

"Ready?" Sam was by my side.

I nodded. Something jagged was clogging my throat.

We'd agreed that Sam would come up with an excuse to gather his crew together at the bow of the ship for a meeting. If anyone asked where I was, he'd tell them I was busy inside with some research he'd asked me to do.

While they were all distracted, I would jump off the stern, swim to Noah's ship, find Shona, and hopefully discover a way to free her from her cage. If I couldn't manage it, at least I'd be able to let her know that she wasn't on her own. I was here, Sam was on our side, and neither of us would give up on her. We'd get her out of there.

"Good luck," Sam said roughly. He stood there, by my side, for another half a minute without saying anything.

I turned to him. My face was a hairbreadth away from his. "What?" I asked.

He leaned forward and whispered, "This."

Then he kissed me.

Almost immediately, he turned away. As he went to call his meeting, I shook myself and tried to get ready to jump off the boat to go rescue Shona, but my mind was racing.

What had just happened? Had Sam actually done that? And had I really let him?

He just wanted to wish me luck. It didn't mean anything. And I didn't even like it.

Maybe if I told myself the same thing enough times, I might believe it.

This was it. Everyone was busy; no one was looking: it was time to go.

I clambered down the ladder attached to the back of the ship. It took me to just above the water level.

One last look. All clear.

As softly and quietly as I could, I let go with one hand, leaned as far down as possible—and jumped.

I landed in the water with a small splash and turned to swim straight down. I dived lower and lower, kicking with my legs and reaching wide with my arms.

As I neared the sandy seabed, I could feel the change spreading through my body. I stopped holding my breath as I felt gills take over the job of being underwater. I stopped kicking my legs as they stiffened and straightened and turned into a tail.

And I stopped worrying about the world above the water. I looked down at my mermaid body. I was ready. I had a job to do.

I flicked my tail and swam toward Noah's ship.

"Shona! Are you there? Can you hear me?"

I'd reached Noah's ship and called through the water as I swam around it, looking for her cage.

And then I saw it—right at the back of the ship. A long chain leading down to a cage. The cage was way below me, deep down, almost on the seabed.

I flipped over and dived down.

I could see her! Just a bit farther below me.

"Shona!" I wanted to scream with relief. I wanted to hug her tighter than I'd ever held anything. But I couldn't, as she was still inside the cage. It was bouncing gently on the seabed, swaying with the current.

I swam down to the bars that surrounded her.

"Emily!" Shona swam up to the side of the cage and poked her arms through the tiny gaps.

I took both of her hands in mine. "Shona! Are you OK? Are you hurt?" I asked.

"I'm fine. Honestly. Just a bit shaken." I could see Shona's eyes had filled with tears—but I could also see she was trying to be brave, so I didn't mention it.

"What happened? How did they catch you? Were you with my dad? What did they do to you?" The questions burbled out of me in a mangled mess.

"They caught me yesterday," Shona said. "We

193

stayed another night at the island after you'd gone. Then, yesterday afternoon, we swam to where Neptune's transportation was supposed to meet us, but we couldn't find the chariot. Your dad went off to see if he could find out what was happening. He told me to stay where I was in case it came. While I was swimming above the water, looking around, the ship came by."

"Oh, Shona!"

She went on, her voice numb, almost lifeless. "I saw Aaron on board so didn't think I was in danger, but in about a second, I was trapped. They grabbed me and bundled me into a cage before I knew what was going on."

"Did my dad come back?"

She shook her head. "I didn't see him again. I don't know what happened to him. I don't know if he got away, if he found Neptune's chariot, or what."

Shona looked like she was seriously going to cry now. Well, she'd looked like she was going to cry the whole time we'd been talking. Now she looked like she was going to collapse in a crumpled heap and cry till she'd raised the sea level with her tears.

"I'm going to get you out of here," I said. "I promise."

"What are you doing here, anyway?" Shona asked. "Did you get captured, too?"

Where was I supposed to start? "I'll explain everything when we've got more time," I said. "But I'm here to help—and right now, you are my priority."

Shona let go of my hands and pulled at the bars of the cage. "This thing is locked solid. I don't know how we'll manage it."

I swam around the cage, studying it from every angle, looking for a weak link. "There's got to be a way of getting it open," I murmured as I swam. "We have to get you out of here before they come for you."

Shona opened her mouth to say something else. Then she stopped.

"Shona, what is it? Are you OK?"

She nodded. "I have to tell you something," she said. "I don't want to. I wish it weren't true. But you need to know."

Shona looked so upset I couldn't even begin to imagine what she was going to say.

"It's OK," I said. "Whatever it is, you can tell me."

She hesitated for a moment. Then in a quiet voice, she said, "It's Aaron. He's changed. I think Noah has turned him."

I dropped my head. "I saw him with Noah," I said. "I didn't want to believe what I was seeing."

"I wouldn't have believed it either if I hadn't

seen and heard him for myself when they pulled my cage up to check on me," Shona agreed. "I thought he must be pretending, but the way he's been laughing and joking with them, I'm just not sure."

Even though I'd seen for myself that what Shona was saying was true, I could still barely believe it. It was unthinkable; it was horrendous; it was—

CLANK! CLANK! CLANK!

The cage was moving!

"Emily! They're pulling me up!" Shona's face was white.

She swam around and around in her cage as I looked for a way to get it open. *"Hurry!"* she begged.

"I'm trying," I said, pulling and yanking uselessly on a padlock that held a bolt across the door. "I just can't see how to get you out of this thing. Shona, I don't know what to do!"

The cage rose higher and higher.

"Maybe I could try to squeeze through the bars," Shona suggested. "If I go arms first, you could pull me, and I'll swish hard with my tail and—"

"Shona, you'll never get your head through them. The gaps are only a tiny bit wider than your arms. You'll get stuck, and then we'll be in even more—"

CLANK! CLANK!

Shona fell on the floor as the cage tipped and jerked upward.

I swam up alongside her. We were nearly at the surface now.

"Emily, please! Do something!"

"I'm sorry," I whispered to Shona.

"It's not your fault," she said. "None of this is your fault. OK?"

I fought back a tear as I nodded. The cage clanked upward again. One last jolt and it broke through the surface of the water.

I had nothing to lose. Shona was all that mattered now. If she was being transferred to the pirate king's ship, they could take me with her.

Steeling myself for whatever was about to happen, I flicked my tail, swam as hard as I could, and broke through the water to face our captors.

"Aaron!"

Aaron was leaning over the back deck of the ship, hauling on the winch that had lifted the cage up.

He spun around toward me. He looked as shocked to see me as I was horrified to see him.

"Emily! What are you doing here?" he asked.

"What am *I* doing? What am—?" I could barely speak. "How *could* you?" I burst out. "How could you do it, Aaron?"

Aaron glanced around, then locked off the winch and came to the edge of the deck. "Do *what*?" he asked in a whisper.

"Join Noah! Become one of his crew. Please, please, tell me I've got it wrong."

Aaron stared at me. His eyes turned from shock to anger, then—I didn't know what. Hurt?

"Surely you know me better than that!" he hissed.

I flicked my tail to tread water. "I—I thought I did," I replied. "I mean—I do. Of course I do. But it just looks so—"

"Convincing?" Aaron cut in. "That's the whole point!"

Shona had swum to the top of the cage so her head was above water. Aaron looked down at her. His face was even paler than usual. "Shona, you didn't actually think I'd joined Noah's crew, did you?"

Shona flicked her head. Droplets of water sprinkled around her. "I . . . I didn't *want* to. You just looked so happy and at home with them all. It looked so real."

"Good!" Aaron said. "It was *supposed* to look

real. I figured it was my only way to survive—or be of any use to you. It was either go undercover, pretend to be a convert, and cozy up with Noah, or be treated like a prisoner by one of the meanest men I've ever met." He looked from Shona to me and back again. "Surely you know I'd never betray you guys? You're my best friends in the world!"

I reached for his hand. "I'm sorry, Aaron. I should never have doubted you."

Aaron looked at my hand for a moment. Then he covered it with his. "I guess I must have looked pretty awful up there," he said with a grimace. "I'm sorry I scared you. Both of you."

"I'm sorry I doubted you," Shona added.

"All right. It's OK. I'm just glad you know the truth now." He looked around again. "Look, we haven't got long."

"Got long for what?" I asked.

"For what I came here to do!" He reached into his pocket and pulled out a bunch of keys. "I managed to find these."

"What are they?" I asked.

"A spare set of keys. I found them in a cabinet in Noah's office. Which I only managed to get into because he trusts me."

I winced at his words. How could I have doubted him?

Aaron held the keys out. "Shona, I'm going to let you out!"

"You're freeing me?" Shona gulped.

"Of course I'm freeing you!" Aaron replied. "What else would I be doing? I just need to find the right one and you'll be on your way. I'll stay here and cover for you."

"Wait," Shona said. "I've got a better idea."

"What's that?" Aaron asked.

Shona grinned at us both. "We *all* escape. Aaron, dive in and join us. We unlock the cage and all three of us swim away!"

Neither of us replied for a minute. I didn't know what to say. I mean, Shona's idea was brilliant. Of *course* it was. This was the perfect moment. So what was holding me back? And, in fact, now that I thought about it, what was holding Aaron back?

"How come you haven't tried it already?" I asked.

"What? Leave Shona in a cage and swim away?" Aaron asked. "I've told you, I'd never—"

"No, I mean, how come you haven't tried this before? Unlocked the cage and both of you swim away?"

Aaron glanced around nervously. "Emily, you don't know what it's like on this ship. You saw the way Noah shouted at everyone earlier? He's like that over the slightest thing. He doesn't trust

200

anyone; he blows up over nothing. He makes us do everything in pairs so there's always someone watching all of us. He even has people patrolling the cabins all night to make sure no one is secretly plotting against him. You don't get a minute to yourself, never mind a chance to jump ship."

"How come you're on your own now?" Shona asked.

Another glance around. "Because we've been given an hour off, and Tom—the guy I'm paired with today—fell asleep in the sunshine. It's literally the first chance I've had to get away."

"So let's do it," Shona repeated. "All three of us. Let's go. Right now. What's stopping us?"

Shona was right. What *was* there to stop us? No one was watching us. As far as any of them knew, Shona was trapped in a locked cage, and Aaron and I were a normal boy and girl who wouldn't stand a chance of getting away from the pirate ships undetected.

At least, as far as *almost* all of them knew.

Sam knew different. Sam was expecting me back.

But why should that stop me?

Aaron beamed at us both. "Shona's right. Let's do it now! There's safety in numbers. Let's go. Are you ready, Emily?"

"I . . ." I said weakly. How could I *not* be ready?

It was ridiculous even to consider it. Aaron and Shona were the only ones I cared about around here. Sam meant *nothing* to me. I didn't owe him anything.

But if all of that were true, why did it feel like a lie?

"OK, let's go," I said, forcing enthusiasm into my voice and hating myself for the fact that it wasn't totally real.

Aaron sat on the edge of the deck, took off his shoes, and was about to jump in when—

"Aaron!"

I instinctively darted around to the side of the ship, out of sight.

A boy joined Aaron on the deck. One of Noah's crew. He looked a couple of years older than Aaron. He was wearing torn black jeans and a green tank top. He had a freckled face and strawberry-blond straggly hair, a couple of earrings in one ear, a stud through his chin.

"What're you doing, man?" he asked.

The keys were on the deck next to Aaron, just out of the boy's sight. Aaron stood up, grabbing the keys as he did and holding them behind his back.

Aaron cleared his throat. "Hey. Tom. I was . . ." he began. "I was just checking on the cage. I saw the chain moving around and had a feeling something wasn't right." As he spoke, he pointed at the winch. "So I brought the cage up to check on it."

"And . . . ?" the boy asked, folding his arms and narrowing his eyes at Aaron.

"And it was fine," Aaron said.

Tom stood there, arms folded, scowling at Aaron for a moment. "I know exactly what you were doing," he said in a low voice.

No! This was it. Game over. Aaron had turned white.

Then Tom burst into a wide grin and he punched Aaron on the shoulder. "You just wanted to have a look at the cute mermaid, didn't you! Come on. Admit it!"

Aaron forced a laugh and nodded enthusiastically. "You got me," he said. "I figured it wouldn't do any harm to have a quick look close up."

Tom started to walk away. "Wait till I tell the boys," he said over his shoulder. "Aaron's in love with the mermaid." He threw his head back and laughed. "Come on, pal. Let's winch it back down again and head back to the others. Noah says he wants to talk to us all."

Tom was trudging across the deck. Aaron waited another moment, then he turned and bent over the railing. He was holding the keys out. "Quick," he hissed. "Take them. Let Shona out— get away, both of you."

"What about you?" I asked.

Aaron shook his head. "I'll be fine. I'll escape. I'll find a way."

I thought of what Sam had said about the punishment he'd face if he ran away. Would Aaron face even worse? That was assuming he ever managed to slip Noah's attention for long enough to even think about it.

"Emily, I've got to go." And with that, Aaron held out his hand and threw the keys into the water. They landed with a splash just in front of me.

Aaron stood up and called across to Tom. "Hang on, man. I'll give you a hand with that," he said.

I didn't hear anything else. I couldn't risk staying around to listen. The keys to Shona's cage were sinking fast. If I didn't dive down to get them, any chance of freeing her would sink just as quickly.

"Be careful, Aaron," I whispered.

And then I ducked under the water, grabbed the keys, and swam over to release Shona from her cage.

Chapter Sixteen

I worked frantically at the padlock. For all we
knew, Noah could be calling his crew together
to give them instructions to transfer Shona to his
father immediately.

I knew we wouldn't have long to get Shona
away from here.

"None of them seem to be working," I said,
my hands shaking as I tried the fourth key on the
ring. It didn't fit.

"Keep trying," Shona said, swishing her tail

nervously as she gripped the bars between us. "It's got to be one of them."

The fifth one didn't fit either. Nor did the one after it. There were only three keys left. What if Aaron had picked up the wrong set of keys?

What if Noah discovered they were missing and was calling his crew together to find and punish the person who'd taken them?

I forced all the worried thoughts out of my mind and concentrated on the task in front of me.

Two more keys to go. I tried the first of them. . . .

It worked! *It worked!*

"Shona! We've found it!" I cried as I turned the key in the lock and the padlock sprung open. I yanked it off the chains wrapped around the bars. As the chains fell away, I pulled the door open.

Shona swam out of the cage and straight into my arms. "Thank you, thank you, thank you!" she burst out. "I thought I was going to die in there."

"Well, thanks to Aaron, you're safe now," I replied.

"I feel so bad for ever doubting him," Shona said, letting me go and treading water with her tail.

"Yeah, me too," I admitted. "But he did it for you. And now you're free—so, go. Swim away!"

Shona looked confused. "What about you? Aren't you coming with me?"

"I . . ." Shona was right. I should go with her. But I couldn't—not yet. Not while I knew Aaron was stuck on that ship with awful Noah watching his crew's every move. "I'm not going anywhere till Aaron's safely away from here," I said. It was why I was here in the first place: I wasn't ducking out of my responsibility to him now.

Shona nodded. "I understand."

"Will you find your way out of here?" I asked.

She smiled. "It's the ocean," she said. "It's my home. I'll always find my way."

I threw my arms around her. "Be careful," I said, hugging her tightly.

Shona hugged me back just as tightly. "You too. You're absolutely sure about this? I hate leaving you."

"I'll be OK," I said. "I promise you. Please, get away from here. Get as far away as you can. And make sure my parents are OK."

"OK," Shona said reluctantly. And with one more hug, she turned away, flicked her tail, and swam off, out to sea.

I watched her swim away. Then I prepared myself for whatever was waiting for me back on Sam's ship. We needed to win this contest more than ever now. Sam *had* to become pirate king. It was our only chance of getting Aaron away from

Noah. And after the risk he'd just taken to free Shona, there was no way I was leaving this contest till I'd done the same for him.

I reached Sam's ship and pulled myself up at the stern, out of sight, while I waited for my tail to disappear and my legs to return.

Kat appeared as I was getting up. "Emily!" She bounded toward me and flung her arms around me. "Omigosh, I'm so glad you're OK!" She released me from the hug and stood back to look at me, clutching my arms with her hands. "Guys! Emily's back!" she yelled.

A minute later, Ana had joined us and given me an equally huge hug. A couple of the boys joined them. They were all grinning so widely you'd think . . .

What *would* you think? That they cared? Maybe they did. Even if it did seem a bit odd that they were responding so enthusiastically when they didn't know I'd even been gone.

Or did they?

"Where's Sam?" I asked.

Luke jabbed a thumb behind him. "He's at the bow, straightening up the ropes."

"Do you mind . . . ?" I asked.

Ana laughed. "Go for it. We'll join you in a bit. You need to catch us up on everything!"

As I made my way along the deck to Sam, I couldn't help wondering what exactly she meant by *everything*. Did she know? Had Sam told them about me?

He couldn't have. There's no way I'd have got a reception like that if they knew what I was.

I clambered over ropes and hatches, wound my way along the side of the ship, and climbed up the steps to the front deck.

My heart did a really annoying skip as Sam looked up. His face, slightly grimy, as usual, was frowning in concentration—until he saw me. Then it changed completely. He dropped the ropes he was holding, smiled so brightly it was as though the sun had just come out behind his eyes, and jumped up.

A second later, his arms were around me. "You're back!" he exclaimed in my ear, squishing me so hard I could barely breathe, let alone reply.

I hesitated for a moment, then hugged him back. We didn't move for a couple of seconds. Then I started to feel awkward, so I wriggled out of his grasp.

As I pulled away, he was still grinning. "I thought I'd never see you again," he said. "I thought you were—well, I don't even want to think about what I thought."

He sat and patted the space next to him. "Come. Sit. Tell me everything."

So I did.

I told him how Noah watches his crew like a jailor. I told him about Aaron taking a massive risk for Shona. I told him she was free, she'd escaped. I told him I was depending on him to keep his part of the bargain to help me get Aaron safely away from Noah. That this was the reason I had come back, rather than swim away with Shona when I had the chance.

"I'm glad you're back," Sam said when I'd talked myself dry. "Is that selfish of me?"

I shook my head. "I'm glad to be back too," I said, shocked by how much I meant it.

He smiled. "And I'm going to do everything I can to help you, and help Aaron. I've made a promise, and I want you to see how seriously I take that. I'll make sure the whole crew is on board with it too."

"Sam, about the crew . . ." I began. "I have a question."

"What is it?"

I was suddenly embarrassed. If I asked the question, it meant having to be OK with the answer. Still, I had to know.

"Have you told them . . . ?"

"Told them what?"

"About me? About . . . what I am?"

Sam burst out laughing. "Well, it turns out I didn't have to. Not all of them, anyway. Ana and Kat had somehow figured it out already—don't ask me how."

"Really?" I thought about the reception they'd both given me. All those hugs—despite the fact that I was a mermaid! Weren't they supposed to be disgusted and horrified by me?

"Really! And . . . I hope you don't mind, but I told the boys, once you'd gone. They were asking so many questions I just thought the truth was the best way to answer them. I wanted them to hear it from me, not from some kind of rumor mill."

"And?"

Sam shrugged. "Luke and Hal were completely cool about it. Dean was a bit weird—but, then, Dean is a bit weird about most things, so I wouldn't worry about it. Turns out *no one* really understood why we were supposed to hate mermaids so much anyway. And it seems that no one actually does!"

I laughed. "Wow," I said. "That's . . ." I paused. Then I said, "That's swishy!"

"Swishy?"

I couldn't help smiling back. "Yeah," I said. "Swishy."

Sam grinned. "Swishy it is!"

He stood up and held out a hand to pull me up too. I got up and followed him back to the ropes. "Come on. Give me a hand," he said, looking at his watch. "Dad has summoned us to meet in an hour for the final challenge. Apparently, this one has two parts to it, so two points."

"Which means you could still win."

"Exactly. And that's precisely what I plan to do."

"I'll do everything I can to help make it happen," I said.

"I know." Sam grinned widely. "And *when* I win, I promise you, I will free Aaron."

Sam had been gone more than an hour. He'd taken the tender over to his dad's ship to get the instructions for the final challenge.

Ana was drawing a tattoo on my arm with a special ink. It looked like tar. Smelled like it, too. "Lasts longer than henna and doesn't hurt like a needle," she'd said when I asked if she'd do one for me.

I didn't know what picture I wanted, so she'd said she'd "draw from the heart and see what happens."

It had been about half an hour when she sat back and examined her work. "Done," she said. "Take a look."

I twisted my arm to study the picture. Two ships' anchors crossed over each other, skull-and-crossbones style. Leaning against the anchors was a mermaid. Her tail was looped around the anchors and flopped over the top of them.

A pirate mermaid.

"It's beautiful," I gasped. I was too choked up to say anything else.

"It's pretty cool," Ana agreed. "If I say so myself!"

Just then, Hal appeared in front of us. "Sam's back. Gather around," he said.

I pulled down my sleeve carefully so as not to smudge my tattoo, and Ana and I went to join the others, to find out what the pirate king had in store for us next.

"Read it again," Kat insisted.

Sam cleared his throat and read again from the piece of paper he'd brought back with him.

"We pirates know, deep in our bones, that all that glitters is not gold.

But yet we know most true as well, that diamonds
  shall reward the bold.
So follow the diamonds as they swim away into the
  darkest night.
They'll lead you to the Trident's Treasure. Let them
  be your guiding light.
Work as a team, be brave and strong, and when
  you think your way is near,
Take three deep breaths, prepare yourself, then five,
  four, three, two, one — you're here."

"This is it," Luke said. "The final test. We have to find the treasure."

"The Trident's Treasure," Ana added.

"And this is all we're getting by way of a clue," Dean added, shaking his head. "What use is that? It doesn't even make sense. Diamonds swimming? What on earth is that supposed to mean?"

"We don't know yet," Luke said wearily. He was obviously getting as fed up with Dean's attitude as the rest of us were. "But that's the whole point. It's not going to be easy, is it?"

"It's *supposed* to be a challenge," Sam agreed. "Finding the Trident's Treasure is the thing that's going to prove either me or my brother worthy of taking on the family business. And it's about time we *all* decided we are up to this challenge, and we are going to *win* it."

No one said anything. Even Dean didn't argue with him this time. "OK, boss," he said with a shrug. "What's the plan?"

Sam's eyes widened for a moment. Dean had never called him "boss" before. He recovered quickly and carried on. "Crystal Bay is one of hundreds of bays around here. We have to find the one that will lead us to Halfmoon Castle."

"Why not just try them all?" Kat asked.

Sam shook his head. "We haven't got time. The sun's already starting to go down."

"So?" I asked.

"Dad told us that in order to win, one of us has to find it before the sun has risen tomorrow."

"We have less than a day?" Ana asked.

Sam looked at his watch. "We have barely twelve hours," he said.

No one said anything. What, exactly, *could* we say?

"Look, if we work together, we can do it. We just have to find Halfmoon Castle. We found Crystal Bay, so we can find this too," Sam went on. "We know that the Trident's Treasure is in there somewhere. Oh, and Dad said he had one more clue for us. He told us that once we get inside, we're to look for a red door. If we get the wrong room, we fail. Time is against us, so let's stay focused. The first thing we need to do is try to unravel the clues in the poem."

215

He passed the piece of paper around so we could all look at the poem.

"It doesn't make sense," Kat said. "It says we need to find the diamonds first—and they'll lead us to the treasure. But, surely, diamonds *are* treasure."

"That's what I was thinking," Dean agreed. "So we have to find treasure that will lead us to more treasure. Seems a bit stupid to me."

"Look, let's put a couple of sails up and start moving," Sam instructed. "We'll just edge slowly around the coastline. Keep looking out at all times, and keep studying the poem till we make a breakthrough, one way or the other. Everyone OK with that plan?"

We all agreed, and then we set to work. Luke and Dean went to put up the sails. Kat took the helm. The rest of us studied the words of the poem Jakob had given to his sons.

We sailed slowly around the coast as the light faded more and more rapidly. Soon we were sailing in pitch darkness. Kat switched on the center light on the mast, and we huddled around it as we moved slowly through the water.

We talked about the poem. We studied it. Read it over and over. We brainstormed, we argued, we scratched our heads. Every now and then, someone would come up with a thought that sounded good—until someone else shot it down a minute later.

My head was spinning. "I'm going to take a walk," I said to Sam. "I need to be alone, give my brain a chance to think."

"OK, be careful. Hold on to the rails. It's pitch-black away from the light," Sam said.

"I'll be fine," I said.

And then I stepped away from the group and felt my way along the edge of the ship.

Sam was right. Once I was away from the light in the center of the ship, it was *really* dark.

Wait. Didn't the poem say something about the darkest night?

I moved even farther away from the light, making my way up to the very front of the ship. After stepping carefully over lockers and between ropes, I leaned on the railing and looked out.

It was breathtaking. Above me, the sky was huge, pitch-black, and crammed with so many stars it was almost like watching fireworks: the ones with the rockets that shoot straight up into the sky and explode into a thousand bright-white lights.

I couldn't stop staring. The longer I looked, the more stars I could see.

"Amazing, isn't it?" Sam's voice startled me.

I jumped and turned to face him.

"Sorry, didn't mean to startle you," he said. "Mind if I join you?"

I shuffled over and Sam stood next to me, holding on to the railings and leaning out.

"Where's the moon?" I asked.

"It's a half-moon tonight," he said. "The moon won't rise until past midnight. That's why it's so dark."

"Half-moon?" I replied. "When we're looking for Halfmoon Castle. Is that significant?"

Sam shrugged. "My brain is shot right now," he said. "I have no idea what's significant and what isn't."

I laughed. "I know what you mean. That's why I had to get away."

"Me too."

We looked out together in silence for a moment. Above us, the sky, packed with stars; below us, the sea, just as dark, and . . .

Wait.

"Sam." I pulled on his arm and pointed down at the water. "What's that?"

He looked where I was pointing. "What's what?"

The boat was moving almost silently through the water. The only sound was a humming through the sails and the gentle clatter of the halyards against the mast.

Below us, the bow spread small waves as it

dipped through the swell. Each time the hull bounced on a wave, the splash seemed to light up the water behind it. I waited till it happened again.

"That!"

Sam watched for a while. "Oh, that. It's bio-luminescence," he said.

"What's bioluminescence?"

"It happens at night. You see it on the water." He shrugged. "I've never been totally sure how it happens. Plankton, I think. Tiny organisms that get lit up by the movement of water. It happens when it's really dark."

"Like tonight."

"Yeah. Beautiful, isn't it?"

"It's incredible." I'd never seen such a sight, at least not to this extent. I'd seen tiny lights in the water from the boat before, but never like this. It was mesmerizing. Thousands of tiny sparkles of bright-white light, flashing on the surface, like . . .

A spark of realization ran through my chest. "Sam!"

"Huh?" He replied without looking up. He was as mesmerized by the bioluminescence as I was.

"Sam, they look like jewels," I whispered. "They look like *diamonds*."

"Yeah, they do," he replied dreamily. He hadn't caught on to what I was thinking. I'd have to spell it out.

"Sam. Follow the diamonds. That's what the poem said. Could it possibly mean . . . these?"

I was grasping at straws. I knew I was, even as I said it.

Sam turned toward me. I could see him thinking for a moment. Then he shook his head. "Surely not," he said. "I mean—any pirate knows about bioluminescence."

"And knows about diamonds too," I added.

"Exactly. No pirate would think this was anything special. They've probably seen it every night of their lives. Plus, look." He pointed at the lights. "They come from movement. They flash up *behind* the wave. The poem said the diamonds will *lead* us. These are *following* us."

"You're right," I agreed.

"Unfortunately," Sam said. He let go of the railings. "I'm going to head back to the others. See if anyone's come up with anything," he said. "Be careful out here, OK?"

"I will. I'll be back soon."

As he started to walk away, I kept looking down at the water. Even if it didn't have anything to do with our challenge, I still couldn't tear my eyes away from the sparkling lights. They were entrancing. Magical.

But as I looked, I saw something else. Something new. The lights were changing shape.

I leaned on the railings and craned my neck to stare more closely.

There! There it was again!

I could hardly believe what I was seeing.

"Sam!"

He'd disappeared into the darkness. "Sam!" I called a bit louder.

"What is it? You OK?" he called back from somewhere farther along the ship. I didn't dare look away from the water. "Come back!" I shouted.

A moment later, Sam was back by my side. "What is it?" he asked. "What's the matter?"

I pointed at the water, at the sparkles. I could hardly speak.

"What am I looking at?" Sam asked, scanning the water.

"Wait. You'll see it," I whispered.

And then it came again. A shape, moving through the bioluminescence.

"What in the . . . ?" Sam began. He couldn't finish. We stared together. I knew exactly what we were staring at.

A dolphin, swimming through the bioluminescence. It looked as if it were made out of diamonds.

"I've never seen anything like it," Sam murmured.

As the dolphin swam through the bioluminescence, the lights took on its shape. A beautiful dolphin, made of magical jewels.

It swam up to the surface, as if it wanted to see if we were watching. Then the dolphin dived back down, spreading a feast of glitter all around it.

"Sam, look — it's swimming away from us."

"Well, at least we saw it," he said. "What a sight. Now, I'd better get on with—"

"Sam!" I stopped him.

He turned to me, met my eyes. "What is it, Emily?" he asked, almost impatiently.

"The dolphin! It made sure we were watching, and now it's swimming away . . ."

"Em, we need to get on with the challenge. It's getting late and we're running out of—"

"Sam! The dolphin *is* the challenge."

I waited a beat for him to register what I was saying. Then I quoted the poem I'd read over and over so many times I now knew it by heart.

"So follow the diamonds as they swim away into the darkest night.
They'll lead you to the Trident's Treasure. Let them be your guiding light."

I watched Sam's eyes turn from clouded confusion to realization. "The dolphin . . ." he began.

"You know what this means, don't you? The diamonds. The poem. It's not talking about *real* diamonds. It's not real treasure." I pointed down to the dolphin, still staying within our sight, pulling ahead a tiny bit, its shape magically lit up by a thousand sparkles. "It's the dolphin," I finished. "It's come to help us. It will lead us there."

"Emily," Sam breathed. "How did I ever manage without you?"

I was too embarrassed to reply.

"Come on," he continued. "Quick. Let's tell the others. We'll organize a watch. Have someone watching the dolphin and reporting on its position at all times. We'll sail through the night; we'll work nonstop."

"No one will want to sleep now," I said, adrenaline coursing through me as I followed Sam back to the others.

"No sleep, no rest," Sam agreed.

"Till we find Halfmoon Castle," I added. "And win the contest."

223

Chapter Seventeen

We sailed through the night, each taking turns with all the jobs: at the helm; at the bow, watching the dolphin; on the deck setting the sails; making snacks and drinks to keep us going.

No one mentioned being tired. Even Dean worked like the rest of us and didn't complain once.

We were a fine-tuned, superefficient team. Led by a magical, beautiful dolphin.

I was on watch at the front with Ana when the dolphin began to slow its pace. I called back to

Luke, who was at the helm, and he instructed the others to adjust the rigging.

The dolphin wasn't just slowing. It was stopping. It swam around in front of the boat, backward and forward, under the bow, diving in the waves still breaking, as the ship slowed. The jewels of bioluminescence still sparkled.

"What are you trying to tell us, beautiful creature?" Ana asked.

I could now see fairly clearly in the moonlight. We were in a tiny bay, much smaller than Crystal Bay. There was no beach here. From where we were, it looked as though the bay was surrounded by sheer cliffs.

Why had the dolphin brought us here?

For the first time, a sliver of doubt wriggled through my mind. Had we gotten it wrong?

I studied the coastline again. And that was when I noticed something different, right in the center of the cliffs.

"Ana, can you see that?" I asked, pointing at the dark line.

She peered into the darkness with me. "Looks like a crack in the cliffs," she said.

She was right. As I stared harder, I could see that the cliffs were in fact made out of two sections: one on the right, one on the left—divided by a dark chasm in between. It was too small for a ship to get through, and the rocky cliffs looked too dangerous for us to risk sailing much closer.

"Now what?" Ana asked. "It's a dead end."

"No, it's not," I said. I looked back down at the dolphin. I tried something out. Climbing over the bowsprit, I crossed from one side of the deck to the other.

The dolphin swam under the bow to follow me. I crossed back.

The dolphin swam back with me.

"Ana, I think the dolphin is telling me something," I said. "I think I'm supposed to follow it." I pointed at the crack in the cliffside. "The ship can't get through there . . . but I can."

As soon as I'd spoken, the dolphin leaped out of the water, leaping straight up in a pirouette of light. It was telling me I was right.

"Look, stay here. I'll go and investigate. Keep an eye on me," I urged, already pulling off my shoes and stepping over the railings.

"Emily, don't. It's dangerous. You might . . ." Ana began as I slipped into the water.

"I might what?" I asked, treading water as I waited for my tail to form. "Drown? I can't. I'm a mermaid."

Ana put her hand to her mouth. "Just . . . please, be careful," she said.

"I will. Follow us as far as you can. When it

gets too shallow, tell Sam to drop anchor and then wait for my instructions."

"OK, will do," Ana replied.

I turned to give Ana a thumbs-up. Then I dived down into the water, through the bioluminescence. I could feel it light me up, inside and out. I felt as though I were swimming through magical sparkles.

My tail formed and I caught up with the dolphin and prepared myself for whatever was going to happen next.

I realized pretty quickly why the dolphin had stopped in the bay earlier. There was no way the ship could have sailed through to where we were now. Sam and his crew had followed us as far as they were able. Then he'd done as I'd suggested and dropped anchor.

I'd swum on with the dolphin, snaking along thin channels between rocks, navigating through chasms so sharp and narrow that I caught my arms and tail on them a couple of times. Their sides were dark and steep, stretching way up above the surface of the sea and way down to the murky depths of the seabed below.

And then, without warning, the dolphin halted.

"What?" I asked. "Why have you stopped?"

The dolphin nodded at the surface and I followed it up. As we broke through the water, I could see why it had stopped.

In front of us, the cliffside stretched up in an almost vertical wall. At the bottom, a couple of rocky steps led out of the water. Just above them, a dark hole led into the cliff itself.

"In that cave?" I asked.

The dolphin continued to swim around me. I guessed it was my only option.

So I swam up to the cliff edge and pulled myself out of the water. I sat on the steps while I waited for my tail to disappear and my legs to return. While I did, I looked around.

Rocks. Water. Cave. Dolphin. And a bunch of debris that had washed up, presumably from years of neglect. There was a tangled piece of fishing rope, some frayed lengths of driftwood, a few plastic bottles.

I had an idea.

As soon as my legs had come back, I got up and carefully made my way across the rocks to the tangled rope. Working at the tangles and knots, I managed to free most of it. I collected as much of the debris as I could gather. I tied the rope around bottles and logs and pieces of driftwood.

And then I stepped back into the water.

The dolphin was by my side in an instant. Together, we swam carefully along the route I'd taken from the ship. At every point where there were jagged rocks or other dangers, I wrapped the fishing rope around the obstacle, swam back up to the surface, and made sure that one of the pieces of floating debris was above it.

Rock by rock, danger by danger, I'd soon marked out a safe channel for the others to swim ashore from the ship.

"Thank you," I whispered to the dolphin.

And then, with a nod and a snort of water, the dolphin turned, dived down into the water, and was gone.

"Take it slowly," Sam instructed his crew as they dived from the ship and carefully swam across the channel from the ship to the cliffs.

Before they got there, I pulled myself up on a rock that was hidden by darkness. I didn't know why—and I hated that I felt that way—but I was too embarrassed to have them see me transform. I didn't want to risk seeing a look of disgust on anyone's face.

Once my legs had come back, I climbed back

over the rocks to join the others. They were standing in front of the cave, looking in. Sam was at the front. "You all ready for this?" he asked.

"More than ready," Luke replied for us all. "This is what we've come for."

"Let's do it," Sam said. I could just about detect a note of nervousness in his voice. But a different kind of nerves from the ones he'd had when I joined his ship. Those had been about him not feeling he had any authority—and, in truth, he hadn't. This time, it sounded more like the kind of wobble anyone would feel when they were about to lead their trusting crew into a pitch-black hole in the side of a cliff.

The biggest difference was that this time his crew was with him in every way.

"I'll go first," he said. "Emily, I want you to go next in case we get waterlogged and need your help. The rest of you, stay close. Any questions?"

No one replied.

"OK, let's go. We can do this!"

And with that, Sam led the way into the darkness.

I don't know how long we'd been walking. It felt like an hour, but the dark, the narrow winding cave, and the incessant *plip, plip* of water dripping on us all the way messed with our senses, and it could just as easily have been half a day, or five minutes. Every now and then, cracks in the wall allowed the light through. For a few steps we could see clearly; then it would go dark again.

And then we reached the end.

And when I say *end,* I mean an actual, total dead end.

No!

No!

It *couldn't* be!

Sam turned to face me. His expression was horror, disbelief, and dejection, all rolled into one.

"It's over," he said flatly.

The others were still a little way behind us. "Swap places with me," I urged. He squeezed past to let me through, and I went ahead. I felt all around the wall, searching for some kind of gap. Had there been an earthquake? Had something closed it up? Or had we gotten the whole thing wrong?

As I turned to swap places with Sam again, I realized I hadn't felt a *plip* drop down from the ceiling since we'd reached the end of the tunnel.

I looked up to see if anything was different here. And that was when I saw it.

"Sam!" I grabbed his arm.

"What is it?"

I jabbed a finger above me. He looked up and saw it too.

"A trapdoor!" he breathed. "A way in! Em, we've found it! We've really found it!"

Sam grabbed me and started jumping up and down—as much as he was able to in the tight space. I couldn't help laughing.

The rest of the crew was just catching up to us. "What's going on?" Kat asked.

"Emily's found the way in!" Sam burst out. "It's up there!"

Kat looked up. Luke was behind her, then Hal, and the others were just behind them.

"Hal, you're the tallest," Sam said. "Can you reach it?"

Hal shuffled forward and stretched up. "Not quite," he said, straining to reach the ceiling but just missing it.

"Give me a piggyback," I suggested.

Hal looked to Sam. "Do it," Sam said.

Hal leaned down and I pulled myself onto his back. As he stood up, I reached up to the ceiling and pushed at the door.

Creaking and squeaking like something out of an old horror movie, the trapdoor wobbled, moved, and finally swung wide open. We were in!

I climbed from Hal's back onto his shoulders. From there, I pulled myself through the hatch. I'd done it. I was inside! Inside what, exactly, I didn't know yet — and didn't want to think about too much. For all I knew, it could be a room full of massive spiders or rats or —

No. Don't think about it.

I felt around on the damp floor for something that might help the others get up there without breaking Hal's back in the process.

There! Nailed to the floor next to the trapdoor. A rope ladder. It was old, covered in cobwebs, and stiff from lack of use. But it would do.

I gathered it up and held it above the opening. "Watch out," I called down to them. "Ladder coming down!"

I dropped the ladder down to the floor and moved out of the way as, one by one, the crew members climbed up and joined me in the dark, dusty, slightly creepy space.

We peered into the darkness. "All right," Sam said. "Let's split up. All go a different way. First person to find a way out, yell. OK?"

We spread out and felt our way around the pitch-black room. It reminded me of years ago playing "Murder in the Dark" at my old friend Mandy Rushton's house when the power was out. Creeping around in the darkness, hands out in front of me like an extra out of *Scooby-Doo;* it was unnerving.

"Guys!" Ana called. "I've found something."

Following her voice, we made our way over to Ana. She'd found a door. Big wooden thing with a tiny crack in the wood that let sharp slivers of light come through. The door had a bolt across it that was fastened with a combination padlock.

Ana tried the padlock. She turned and shook her head. "Locked. Now what?"

Something was ringing a bell in my mind. Just out of reach, but almost in scratching distance. What was it?

Wait. The poem. That was it! The last two lines — what were they again?

"Ana, how many numbers are on the padlock?" I asked.

"Five. Why?"

I swallowed. "Try five, four, three, two, one," I said.

Sam frowned at me. "Why?"

"The poem," I said simply.

Work as a team, be brave and strong, and when
you think your way is near,
Take three deep breaths, prepare yourself, then five,
four, three, two, one — you're here.

Even in the darkness, I saw Sam's eyes open
so wide the whites were round balls. "Of course!
Take three deep breaths, prepare yourself, then five,
four, three, two, one — you're here." He indicated for
everyone to come closer. "Are you ready?" he
asked. "Together, three deep breaths. Then, Ana,
do what Emily said."

In the dark silence, we slowly breathed in, then
out. In, then out. In, then out.

Without waiting for further instruction, Ana
turned each dial.

5, 4, 3, 2, 1.

The lock sprung open. She turned to smile at
us all. "We did it," she breathed. "We're in."

Walking through the corridors of Halfmoon Castle,
I had a sense of déjà vu. As though I'd been here
before — but, at the same time, I knew I hadn't.

I knew what it was. It was almost identical to Halflight Castle. Similar enough to feel familiar; different enough to make me question everything.

The floors creaked as we made our way along the corridors. The pictures on the walls seemed to be spying on us. The silence wrapped itself around us like a heavy blanket, hiding us—but smothering us at the same time.

"Remember, we're looking for a red door," Sam said.

Corridor after corridor, staircase after staircase, it felt as if we'd covered the whole place.

"Guys, look!" Dean had wandered off down a short corridor that led off the main one. "Down here!"

We followed him around the corner and saw what he was pointing at. Two doors, one opposite the other. On the left, a blue door, and on the right, a red door.

We'd found it!

Dean stood back to let Sam go in first. Taking a deep breath, Sam turned the handle and opened the red door.

And there it was. Right in front of us. A large room with a faded velvet chaise longue on one side. On the other, two huge windows looking out, with floor-to-ceiling curtains draped on either side. Chandelier hanging from the ceiling. Wooden floorboards, with a rug not quite reaching the edges. And in the middle of the room, a large ornate treasure chest.

Sam strode across the room and stood beside the chest.

I felt as though the next part happened almost in slow motion.

Grinning widely, Sam leaned down, stretched out a hand, and undid the clasp that was holding the chest shut.

He paused for a second, turned to smile at us all, and then opened the lid to reveal . . .

Nothing.

The treasure chest was empty.

Chapter Eighteen

*N*obody spoke.

What was there to say? What *could* we say? What words might stand a chance of expressing the disappointment we were all feeling in that moment?

There were none.

Without another word, Sam slowly closed the lid of the chest. He turned toward us, pulled his shirt straight, flattened down his hair, and cleared his throat.

And then he smiled.

"Thank you," he said. "All of you."

Thank you? What was he thanking us for? We'd failed. We'd lost. Everything we'd done had been in vain!

"Over the last few days, I have gained more than you could ever store inside a treasure chest." Sam sought out my eyes, and when he found them, he smiled even more warmly. "I have learned the value of true friendship, loyalty, and courage."

I couldn't help smiling back.

Sam turned to Luke and Hal. "I have learned what it is to have a strong team around me. To have people who understand their jobs and do them better than I ever could."

Hal scuffed the floor with his feet. Luke grinned.

Sam turned to Ana and Kat. "I have learned from others how to see the whole of a person, to know them without judgment. To make up my own mind about who they may be, not take someone else's prejudice and claim it as my own."

Finally, he turned to Dean. He took a step toward him, held his head high as he looked him in the face. "And I have learned that I must *earn* a person's respect," he said quietly. "Not demand it just because it is expected of them."

The look between them was electric. We all held our breath as we watched them. Dean was the first to break the moment.

"Treasure chests are all very well," Dean said, looking at Sam, "but to be honest with you, the journey to it is what I enjoy most." He stepped forward and held his hand out to Sam. "And you led us on a fine journey. Well done, Captain."

Sam took Dean's hand and shook it.

A couple of the others applauded. Kat even cheered. It was as if we hadn't just lost everything. It was as if we'd won. Maybe, in a way, we had.

And then a sound changed the mood in a split second.

I heard it first. "Hey! Shhh!"

Hal and Ana were nearest to me. The others were still cheering and whooping. "What is it?" Ana asked.

"There's something going on in the corridor."

"Guys!" Hal hissed. "Stop what you're doing— now!"

The others stopped and listened. There it was again. It was unmistakable. Feet stomping along the corridor.

"There's someone out there," I said. "And they're heading this way."

We all turned to Sam.

"We haven't got time to get away," he said. "We'll have to hide." He pointed to the windows. "Quick, everyone, get behind the curtains."

I kicked the door closed to give us another

few seconds as we ran to the windows. With four heavy curtains, there was plenty of space for us all to cram ourselves behind them.

We'd just gotten ourselves in place when the door flew open and the footsteps came charging into the room.

"Ah, ha-ha-ha-ha-ha! My brother is such a fool!"

Noah!

"First he leads us here without even realizing it. Then he fails to find the room with the treasure chest in it!"

"His loss; your gain," one of his crew members said.

"As usual," Noah replied. "Now, then, stand back, men. Give me plenty of space as I take my prize."

From where I was standing, I could just see Noah as he stepped toward the chest. I pulled myself back to stay hidden. Not that he was watching us. He only had eyes for the chest.

Noah leaned down toward the chest. "Trident's Treasure, you are MINE!" he boomed as he opened the chest.

There was a split second of silence.

And then—

"WHAT IS THE MEANING OF THIS?" Noah roared.

"What is it?" one of his crewmen asked. "What hap—"

"Don't you dare speak to me, you worthless waste of space!" Noah yelled at him.

He turned to his crew. "How has this happened?" he asked. "Who let this happen? Which one of you messed up? You're all *useless,* you pathetic, stupid *fools*! You *failed*! All of you. You're all sacked! And as for my spineless, cowardly idiot of a brother . . ."

Sam stepped out of his hiding place.

"What about him?" he asked.

One by one, we all stepped out from behind the curtains and stood next to Sam. I noticed Aaron on the other side of the room. I wanted to run to him, give him a hug, see if he was all right. I had to make do with the tiniest hint of a nod. He gave me an almost imperceptible hint of a smile in reply.

Noah stared at his brother. "You, you . . ." he began. His hair was wild, his eyes even wilder. He had spit at the edges of his mouth; his face was bright red. "You worthless, weak loser." In a flash, he'd crossed the room and started looking behind the curtains. "Where is it?" he asked. "I'll find it. No one will believe you got here first. No one in their right mind would make *you* pirate king."

Noah grabbed at the curtains, almost pulling them off their rails. "Where *is* it?" he demanded more fiercely.

Sam shrugged. "I don't have it," he said calmly.

"Don't have it? Don't have it?" Noah blustered. "Don't lie! Where is it? I'll find it. I'll get it. Dad will never believe you over me!"

Noah ransacked the room, pulling out drawers from a dresser on the far side, yanking up the edges of the rug, muttering to himself as he went, and yelling at anyone who came near him.

Noah, the perfect, smart, neat, smooth-talking son, had completely and utterly lost it.

If we weren't so mesmerized by his strange and outrageous behavior, we might have seen what was happening sooner than we did. As it was, it took a few minutes.

It was one of his crew members who saw it first, a boy standing next to Aaron.

"Um, Noah," he said, so quietly that there was no way Noah would have heard him over his own ranting. Maybe that was the idea. No one in his right mind would have interrupted Noah at that point.

The boy coughed loudly. Noah took no notice. The boy tugged on Aaron's sleeve and whispered something to him.

Aaron glanced behind him and then stepped into the center of the room. "Noah," he said firmly. "Everyone!"

Noah finally stopped what he was doing. Panting and disheveled, he spun around to face Aaron. "What is it?" he barked.

"Look." Aaron pointed to the door.

We all looked where he was pointing. We saw the corridor. The room on the other side of the corridor. The room with the blue door.

The door that the pirate king and his wife had just opened and walked through, as they made their way across the room toward an enormous treasure chest.

"We've been had," Noah hissed.

Sam took a couple of steps toward Noah. "By our own father," he murmured.

For once—maybe for the first time in their lives—the brothers were united as they stood together and stared at the spectacle in the opposite room.

The pirate king had reached the chest. As if he could feel our eyes on him, he turned to face us.

He saw us all staring across the corridor at them and promptly burst out laughing.

"Come on in," he called, waving us across the corridor to join them. "Come. Share the moment with me. It's going to be a good one."

Numb with shock, we shuffled into the room.

"Dad," Noah began. "Has there been a mistake?"

"A mistake?" the pirate king replied. He looked at his wife. "I don't think there's been a mistake. Do you, darling?"

Michele giggled. "Jakob, don't tease the boys," she said as if she were scolding him for refusing to buy them an ice cream, not for completely betraying his own flesh and blood. She pointed at the chest. "Come on. Let's get this thing open."

"All in good time, my dear. All in good time," Jakob replied. Then he turned to his sons. "But first, I suppose you'd like me to explain?"

Noah looked ready to explode.

The pirate king folded his arms across his belly. "I have known of the Trident's Treasure for many, many years. It has long been thought of in our world as little more than a myth. But then, a year or so ago, I came across a collection of poems while visiting the area around Halflight Castle and—shall we say—*relieving* several ships of their cumbersome cargo."

"You stole the poems, in other words?" Sam said.

His father shrugged. "Stole, acquired, obtained— call it what you will."

"Go on," Noah urged, his voice tight and controlled.

"Well, I couldn't make heads or tails of them, but I knew that they had something to do with the Trident's Treasure," Jakob continued. "And one of them directly said that your children had to lead you to it. So I came up with a brilliant idea."

"Trick your sons into finding it for you," Noah said, his words so sharp they seemed to bite at the air.

The pirate king tilted his head in mock concentration. Then: "Yes, that's about right, son," he said.

"And what you said about retiring . . . ?" Sam asked.

The pirate king burst out laughing. "Do I look like someone who's about to retire?"

"So it was all lies?" Sam asked.

His dad frowned. "*Lies?* Oh, I wouldn't call it lies. I prefer to think of it more as motivation." He laughed again. "And it worked. Look at us!" He grinned at his wife.

Michele was laughing almost as much as her

husband. But she at least made a show of feeling bad about it. "Come on, now, Jakob. Don't taunt the boys so much. They've done a good job."

"Oh, yes. They've done a grand job. And I owe you my thanks as well, my beautiful, genius wife."

"What did Mom do?" Sam asked.

"She came up with the idea of leaving out the last two lines of the poem," his dad replied.

"Last two lines?" Noah asked. "What last two lines?"

Jakob shuffled in his pockets. "Wait a minute. I've got the original here somewhere," he mumbled. Shoving aside an expensive watch chain hanging down his chest, he added, "I just need to find it among all my gold! And I'll be adding to that soon." He wiped his eyes, now watering from all his laughter.

How could he be so cruel? How could he act like this toward his own sons? I'd seen some pretty incredible things over the last year or so—but nothing had shocked me like the spectacle I was witnessing right now.

"Ah, found it." The pirate king pulled a piece of paper out of his pocket. Mumbling the first part of the poem under his breath, he traced the paper with his finger as he read the last two lines aloud.

*"You'll see two doors in front of you: one painted
red, one painted blue.
Ignore the red and choose the blue. Your treasure is
in front of you!"*

The pirate king folded up the piece of paper
and put it back in his pocket as everyone in the
room stared at him in silence.

He had tricked his sons into taking a wrong
turn at the last minute, so he could take all the
treasure for himself. It was disgusting. *He* was disgusting.

Even Noah was so stunned he could barely
speak.

"Father," he said in a voice that sounded like
a little boy's. "I — I can't believe you've done this
to us."

The pirate king batted his son's words away.
"Oh, don't worry yourself, Noah. It will all be
yours one day. Everyone knows you will inherit
the family business. But not until I'm good and
ready."

"So Noah still gets to inherit everything?" Sam
burst out. "Even though I got here first? Even
though I won the contest fair and square?"

"The contest didn't mean anything, son!" his
dad exploded. "It was just a way of getting the
treasure for myself — and I knew I had to be led

here by my sons! Haven't you gotten that into your stupid head yet?"

His wife put a hand on his arm. "Jakob," she said tenderly. "Don't be so hard on the boy. It's a disappointment to him."

Jakob shook his wife's hand off. "Well, he needs to get used to disappointment," he said. "He's going to have a lifetime of it. Now, then, let's get this chest open and start enjoying our newfound wealth, shall we?"

As his father began to open the chest, Sam stared at him for another moment. Then he turned and stormed out of the room.

"Sam!" I called to him.

He didn't reply.

I glanced at the crew. Ana gave me a nod. "Go after him," she said.

I followed Sam out of the room. He was half-way down the corridor when I caught up with him.

"Sam. Wait."

He stopped but didn't turn around. I walked around to face him, made him look me in the eyes. His face was steel.

"Why are you so angry?" I asked.

"Are you kidding me?" He pointed down the corridor. "Didn't you see what just went down in there?"

"Yes, I saw it. I saw everything," I said calmly, carefully. "I saw a family of pirates acting like . . . a family of pirates."

Sam gritted his teeth, his breath raging in and out of his nostrils as he continued to stare at me.

"You want to be a part of that?" I asked. "I mean, really? Is that what you want to inherit? Is that how you want to live your life? Like them? Like *that*? Do you really want to be a pirate prince?"

Sam's breathing had begun to calm. His eyes lost their intensity. Finally, he dragged a hand through his hair and breathed out heavily. "No," he said. "It isn't. But what choice do I have?"

I thought about my own situation. My worries about people's reactions to who I was. The fact that I'd almost been ashamed of being a mermaid, just because someone *else* said I should be.

"You have the choice to be yourself," I said. "Regardless of what anyone else wants you to be."

"What if I don't know who that is?" Sam asked.

"Then find out." I leaned forward and put my hand on his chest. "Listen to what's in here," I said, whispering now. "Your gut, and your heart, will tell you what to do."

Sam closed his hand over mine. Without moving his eyes away from mine, even for a millisecond, he said, "My heart knows exactly what it wants me to do."

We stayed like that for—I don't know—a minute? An hour? I couldn't break away.

"Hey, is everything OK out here or do you need—?" Someone had come out into the corridor.

I turned to the voice I knew well. "Aaron!"

I saw his eyes flicker to my hand on Sam's chest, Sam's hand over mine. I snatched my hand away, but it was too late.

"Sorry to bother you," Aaron said.

"Wait!" I called, but he'd already turned and gone back inside.

No!

I turned back to Sam. "I'm going after him," I said.

Sam grabbed my arm. "Emily, wait." He paused for a second; it looked as if he were trying to say something but didn't know how to.

"What is it?" I asked.

Sam swallowed hard, chewed a nail already bitten to the quick, took a couple of breaths. Then he spoke quickly. "Just. Look, think about what you said to me, OK? About what *you* want, what other people want. Before you run—after anyone—just make sure it's what *you* want, not what you think someone else wants from you.

251

Remember our deal on the ship, OK? Will you do that?"

I smiled at Sam, remembering our words. "I will if you will," I said again.

"All right. Come on," he said, striding confidently back to the room where everyone was waiting. "Let's go face the music."

Chapter Nineteen

I let go of Sam's hand just before we reached the door.

"Good luck," I whispered.

He turned to give me a quick smile. "You too."

We walked in as Jakob was opening the chest. He leaned forward and lifted the lid, and none of us could keep ourselves from gasping at the sight. The chest was absolutely packed full of gold, diamonds, jewels of every color and shape, glinting and sparkling and sending sparks of light around the room.

Jakob stared at the treasure for a moment, and then he dived in—hurling his arms into the jewels as if he were launching himself into a pool.

But his joy was short-lived.

A second later, Jakob leaped backward, as if he'd been stung or bitten or something.

"What the—?" he screamed, rubbing his arms and frowning, his face curled up in pain.

"Jakob, whatever is the matter?" Michele sounded disgusted.

"The—the—" Jakob jabbed a hand at the treasure chest. "It bit me!"

"It did *what*?" Michele replied. "Don't be ridiculous." She shoved her husband out of the way and leaned over the chest herself. "Diamonds do not bite," she said as she reached into the chest. "And nor do—ARGH!"

Michele pulled her hand back out of the chest and rubbed her arm. "What on earth is happening?" she asked.

Sam went over to join his parents beside the chest. "There's something on there," he said, pointing to an envelope stuck to the inside of the lid.

"I'm not touching it," Michele muttered. So Sam leaned forward and pulled the envelope off the lid.

He opened the envelope and pulled out a card.

"What does it say, son?" Jakob asked.

Sam read aloud.

"The Trident's Treasure marks the love that
    Neptune and Aurora shared,
And here it shall remain until with its new owner
    it is paired.
Perhaps you'll think these jewels you've found
    have been presented just for you.
Be warned: you'll never touch or own them, lest
    your heart is pure and true."

For a moment, no one said anything. Then Noah strutted across the room.

"Poppycock!" he announced as, like his mom and dad before him, he shoved his hands into the jewels. A second later, like his mom and dad before him, he leaped away, gripping his hand and screaming in pain.

The way he jumped reminded me of something. What was it? My mind whirred back over the events of the last few days—and then I had it. On the dance floor back at the ship. The way Noah had leaped when he was dancing with my mom. Just before Sam had picked something up off the floor.

I pulled on Sam's arm. "Where did you find my mom's necklace?" I asked him.

Sam turned to me, confusion clouding his eyes. "What?"

255

"My mom's necklace. The mermaid. Did you pick it up off the dance floor?"

"I . . . yes."

I stepped forward and spoke to Noah. "You couldn't touch it," I said. Turning to Michele, I went on. "Nor could you. My dad had received it from Neptune as a reward for doing good work." I grinned at Sam. "Sam, I think my mom's necklace is part of this collection. That's why no one else in your family could touch it!"

"I wouldn't want to touch that thing. Mermaids!" Michele muttered, making a face of disgust. I didn't care. What she thought of mermaids didn't matter. She wouldn't hold me back from what I knew was true.

I turned to Sam "You *could* hold it," I breathed. "You're the one with the pure heart. *You* should try touching the Trident's Treasure!"

Sam stepped toward the chest. "You think . . . ?"

I nodded. The others crowded around.

Sam carefully leaned over the chest, skimmed his hands over it, lifted out a necklace. "You're right!" he said, turning to me. "The Trident's Treasure—I've won it after all!"

Jakob strode over to his younger son. "Now, hold on a minute, lad," he said. "Just because you can touch it doesn't make it yours. We'll come to some sort of arrangement. Maybe I'll put you in

256

charge of it. But the family business is still mine, and any jewels you receive while working for me — well, they're mine as well."

Sam looked his dad in the eyes, and then he smiled. "I don't want your family business," he said. "I don't want to work for it. I don't want to be part of it. I don't want anything to do with it."

As he spoke, his shoulders seemed to get higher, as though his words were lifting a burden from them.

"I'm done," Sam went on. "I'm taking the ship I've been given, I'm taking this chest filled with treasure — and I'm out. This chest belongs to Neptune and I intend to return it to him."

"Neptune!" His dad laughed. "Neptune is a mythical creature!"

"No, he isn't," Aaron said from the far side of the room. His voice wobbled as he spoke. "He's real. And if he left the treasure here, then I agree with Sam. It's up to him to decide what to do with it now."

Sam nodded at Aaron. "So we'll find him, and we'll ask him. And while we're at it, we will return the rest of my father's stolen treasures to their rightful owners." Sam turned back to his dad. "Father, it's over," he said. "I'm boarding your ship and I'm taking everything. Everything that isn't yours."

Jakob burst out laughing. "On your own?" he scoffed. "I don't think so."

"I won't be on my own," Sam replied. Then he spun around to look at each of us individually. "Who's with me?"

There was a split second of silence, followed by a shuffling from the far side of the room.

And then Dean stepped forward.

"I am," he said. He marched across the room and stood beside Sam. Sam turned to him with a smile full of gratitude and shock in equal parts.

Luke was next. "With you all the way, Captain," he said as he joined Dean beside Sam. Then Hal came forward. And finally, Ana and Kat. Grabbing my hand as she joined us, Ana said, "You're with us, aren't you?"

I stood with them all. "Of course I am!" I said.

Sam grinned at us all. "OK, I'm done," he began. "I have my team."

"No, you haven't," a voice spoke up from Noah's side of the room.

Aaron!

He stepped away from Noah's crew and crossed the room to stand in front of Sam. "I'd like to join you, if you'll have me," he said.

Sam moved aside so Aaron could shuffle in between him and Dean. "Of course we'll have you," he said, reaching out to shake Aaron's hand. "Welcome aboard."

Another guy stepped away from Noah's crew. "I'd like to come as well," he said, crossing the room to join Sam's crew. Another followed, and then another, then two more.

In the end, Noah—by now speechless—was left with only two crew members, one on either side of him. All the rest had joined Sam.

The atmosphere was electric. Sam turned around to face us. "Welcome to you all," he said. "Thank you for your loyalty, and for your trust. I will work hard to earn and keep your respect as your captain. In return, I will expect the same level of work and loyalty from you. We will be a democracy. We will make decisions together. One person, one vote. We will not steal, we will not lie, we will never use violence. And we will not rest until we have returned everything my family has stolen—and righted the wrongs my family has committed."

It was all too much for Noah. He couldn't stand there listening to it anymore. "You're pathetic," he shouted. "All of you! You'll all come crawling back to me in the end, just you wait."

And with that, he stormed out of the room, his two loyal crew members trailing meekly after him.

Dean turned to face us all. "You heard our captain," he said. "If you don't like what he's said, leave now. Go join Noah before it's too late."

No one moved.

Sam smiled at us all. "Thank you," he said. "I won't let you down." Then he turned to his parents, who had remained shocked into silence throughout the proceedings up to now. Sam stood in front of his mother. Her eyes filled with tears.

"Mother, come with us. Help us make amends," he said, his voice hoarse.

Michele shook her head. "I can't," she said. She didn't even look at him. "It's too late for me."

Sam leaned in and kissed his mother's face, wet with tears. He stepped toward his father to shake his hand. Jakob kept his arms folded. "You shouldn't be doing this, son," he growled. "You'll regret it."

"The only thing I'll regret is letting my family define who I am for another minute," Sam replied. Then he let his arm fall and he turned back to us. "Dean, Luke, can you manage the chest between you?"

A couple of other boys offered to join them, and the four of them heaved it up onto their shoulders.

At the door, Sam turned back to his parents. "Bye, Mother. Bye, Father," he said. Neither of them replied. Jakob's face was stone. Michele's was streaked with tears.

"Come on," I said softly. "Let's go."

Sam turned away from his parents. "Wait," he said to me. He fumbled in his pocket and pulled something out. A thin silver chain was looped around his fingers. "Here," he said. "The first thing we're taking back is your mom's necklace. The second thing is you. I'm going to take you home."

I took the necklace from him. "Thank you," I said, my voice breaking on the tears that had squirmed into my throat.

Sam turned to look at his parents one last time.

"I don't wish you any harm," he said. "And if I see you again, I will be civil. But my mission from now on is to undo every nasty thing you have ever done and to turn our family name into something that good people will respect. If it takes all my life, it will be a life well lived."

As his parents stared numbly at him, Sam turned to me and the rest of the crew. "Come on," he said. "Let's get out of here."

Chapter Twenty

S am led the way along the castle's corridors.
Aaron had squeezed past a couple of boys
from Noah's crew to get to me. He went to take my
hand and found the necklace I was still clutching.
"Here," he said. "Let me do it."

I stopped walking so Aaron could clasp the
necklace closed around my neck. As we set off
walking again, he took hold of my hand. We didn't
say anything as we retraced our steps along the
corridors, down the staircases, through the tunnel,
and back to the bay where our ship was waiting.

Except it wasn't.

Or—well, the ship was there. But it wasn't going to take us around the world delivering stolen goods back to their rightful owners anytime soon.

The sails had been torn to shreds: they lay on the deck, flapping in the breeze; some had already blown off the ship, into the water around it.

The main mast had been attacked so savagely it was broken in half.

The wheel had been ripped out of its place and smashed into three pieces.

Who could do such a thing?

As if we needed to ask.

Noah's ship was already nearly at the horizon. He'd gotten away before us and done this. His parting shot had been one last attempt to undermine his brother.

And it seemed to have worked. Sam leaned against the rocks as he looked around. All the words, all the fighting spirit we'd gathered together less than an hour earlier seemed to have been ripped up and thrown on the wind like the sails.

"Jakob's ship is still here," one of Noah's crew members said. "Maybe we could take that."

Sam shook his head. "I promised no stealing—even from my father. We fetch every piece of stolen treasure from his ship, but the ship itself is his, and I'm not going to start this journey in his footsteps. I need to make my own."

He looked around at the crew. "Can I have some volunteers to collect all the stolen goods from my father's ship?" he asked.

Five or six people put their hands up.

"OK, here's the plan. We'll all make our way to the *Morning Star*," Sam said. "Thanks to Emily, we have a safe route through the water to my ship. From there, you guys will row back here to get the treasure and then across to my father's ship in the tender and gather the stolen treasure. The rest of us will figure out how to get the *Morning Star* away from here."

Sam stepped toward the water's edge. He looked up, found my eyes and raised an eyebrow. I knew what he was asking me. I nodded in reply.

"Follow Emily," Sam said. "She will lead the way."

Aaron was by my side in seconds. "Emily," he hissed. "They'll see you."

I shrugged. "I know."

"I mean, your *tail*. They'll know what you are. What *we* are."

"Half of them know already," I said lightly.

"And the rest?" Aaron asked. "What if they're like Jakob and Noah? What if they're disgusted?"

I laughed as I stepped into the water. "What if

they are?" I replied, realizing just how far on this journey I'd come. How much I'd gained; how much I'd let go of. "That's their problem. Not mine."

And with that, I slipped into the cool water. "Are you coming?" I asked Aaron.

He glanced at the others. Then he grinned and nodded. "OK," he said. "Let's go."

And together we let the water fold around us, let our legs disappear, our worries and fears disappearing with them as our tails formed and we led the way to the *Morning Star.*

We'd boarded the *Morning Star* and half the group was rowing the small tender to gather the treasure.

"What are we going to do?" Sam asked me while no one was listening. "We'll never get this ship moving. It's completely broken."

I shook my head. "I honestly don't know," I said. "We'll figure something out."

I could see Aaron at the back of the ship, chatting with Luke. He looked awkward and shy. My heart went out to him. "Can you give me a minute?" I asked Sam. "There's something I have to do."

Sam saw where I was looking. "Yeah," he said.

I was pretty sure I detected a note of regret in his voice. "Do what you need to do. I won't hold you back."

I made my way to the back. "Hey, Aaron, have you got a minute?" I asked.

Aaron left Luke and we found a quiet spot along the side of the ship.

"You OK?" Aaron asked.

"Yeah. I'm good. Are you?"

Aaron shrugged. "I don't know. It's all a bit . . . weird."

"Weird?" I asked.

"Look, I'm just going to say it. You have feelings for him, don't you?"

My face turned into a furnace. "Feelings for who?"

Aaron made a face.

"For Sam?" I asked.

"It's obvious, Em."

"I don't!" I protested. "I don't have feelings for him. I mean, yeah, feelings of—of friendship. But not . . . I don't . . . ." My words tumbled out of me in a garbled rush. Eventually, I stopped fighting against them. "I don't know," I admitted. "I really don't know."

Aaron nodded sadly.

"You're my boyfriend," I said weakly. I couldn't bear to see him look so crushed.

"But I'm leaving," he said.

"You're still going back to Forgotten Island, then?" I asked.

"My plans haven't changed," he said. "I'm going to go back to Brightport to get things sorted. And then, yes, I'm going back to Forgotten Island. That's where I need to be. Unless . . ." He paused.

"Unless what?"

"Unless you want me to stay in Brightport," he mumbled. "With you."

It wasn't till he said those words that I finally knew what I wanted.

I took his hand in mine. "Aaron," I said. "You've got your life waiting for you at Forgotten Island. I've got mine at home in Brightport. And Sam's got his, traveling around the world righting wrongs. We can't follow each other's paths. We have to find our own."

Aaron laughed gently. "That's deep," he said.

I laughed too. "Yeah. But it's true." I took hold of his other hand. "And you know what else is true, don't you?" I asked.

"I—I think so," he said. "But I don't want it to be."

"I know," I agreed. "Nor do I. But it is. You have to go and I have to stay. On my own. I'm sorry, Aaron, but you and I—I think we're over."

Aaron nodded without lifting his head. He let go of my hand to swipe an arm across his face.

"You'll come visit me, won't you?" he asked.

"Of course I will. And I'll write, and we'll talk. We'll still be friends—if you want to be."

Aaron finally looked up at me. His cheeks were wet. "Of course I want to be," he said.

And with that, he threw his arms around me. As I hugged him back, I let my tears fall onto his shoulder.

"I'm sorry," I whispered into his neck.

"Don't be. It's OK. It's the right thing."

We sat like that for a few moments, holding each other, maybe for the last time. The last time we'd hold each other like that, anyway.

A voice interrupted us. "Um, Emily, Aaron. Sorry to interrupt but . . ."

It was Sam. We pulled apart and stood up. "What is it?" I asked.

Sam was grinning. "You need to see this," he said, beckoning us to the front of the ship.

The rest of the crew was already there, cheering, high-fiving one another, grinning, calling down to someone in the water.

Aaron and I hurried to join them. I looked out to see what they were looking at.

And there, in front of the ship, I saw it.

A huge pod of dolphins. Maybe the one who

had helped us find this place was there; I'd probably never know. In the middle of them was—

"Shona!"

Shona waved at me.

"What are you doing here?" I called.

"I'm your best friend!" she called back. "What did you think? That I'd leave you to deal with this on your own? I'd never do that! Have you seen who else is here?"

I craned my neck to see who she was pointing at. There was someone else in the water. I couldn't see their face from where I was, as they were busy tying a rope onto the other side of the ship.

Then they swam around to my side and looked up.

"Dad!"

"Emily!" Dad's smile was brighter than the three bags of sparkling jewels the boys had already brought over from the pirate king's ship on their first haul. He attached a rope to a cleat on the side, then swam over to me. "You OK?" he asked.

"I'm great!" I said. "Especially now."

"Shona's been amazing. She found me and told me everything that's happened. Together we caught up with the *Sunbeam* and they've said they'll hold their position till they hear from us. They're going to do whatever they can to help you."

"And Mom and Millie?"

Dad grinned. "They're fine. They're on the *Sunbeam* and can't wait to see you."

I was going to see Mom again soon! My heart swelled at the thought.

Dad called across to Shona. "Good to go!"

Shona gathered the dolphins, organizing them into a team and spreading the ropes between them so they could pull us along.

She swam among them and instructed the dolphins to pull the ship around.

"Pull us alongside my father's ship first," Sam called to Shona. "We're collecting all the stolen treasure that's on board. And the first ones we'll be returning are the bags that belong to the people on the *Sunbeam*."

"Will do," Shona called back. Then she dived down and swam with the dolphins as they pulled us through the water.

We'd gathered every stolen item we could find from Jakob's ship and we were ready to leave.

As the dolphins pulled our ship around, Sam and I stood at the back.

"Sam," I said, pointing to the shore. His mom and dad were emerging from the tunnel.

Sam looked across to them.

"You OK?" I asked.

"Yeah."

As the pirate king and his wife reached the end of the tunnel and stepped out onto the rocks, they looked across at their son. For a moment, Jakob's haughty arrogance was gone. In that moment, he looked like a father losing his son. He put an arm around his wife's shoulders and together the two of them watched Sam leave them behind.

Finally, Jakob nodded. I guess he knew when he was beaten. Even if he tried to get to his ship, he was so outnumbered by Sam and his crew that he wouldn't stand a chance of reclaiming the treasure.

Sam nodded back to his dad. His mom clasped a hand across her lips, kissed it, and waved the kiss across to Sam. With the saddest of smiles, Sam did the same back to her.

I slipped my hand into his as the ship turned, as we moved away, as his parents faded into the rocky coastline . . . as we left them behind.

Shona and Dad swam with the dolphins as they pulled our beautiful ship through the winding rocky channels in the bay and out to sea.

Aaron joined Sam in the center of the deck. Together, they were already planning out how to fix the ship.

I watched them, wondering for a moment where it would all end up. Where *we* would all end up. Seeing them working together like that, it was as if they were two parts of me. Aaron, the steady safe harbor in a storm. Sam, the exciting, unknown adventure out at sea. Which one represented the real me?

I laughed to myself. If I'd learned anything on this journey, it was that no one could represent the real me — except myself. I didn't have to decide between them. I didn't *need* either of them to know who I was. I was a bit of both, a bit of neither, and a bit of everything in between. From now on, I would be myself, and if anyone didn't like it — well, that was for them to deal with, not me.

I made my way to the front of the ship. Looking down, I saw that Shona was swimming at the back of the pod of dolphins. Kat was leaning over the front deck, talking to her. They had already become friends.

Everything was linked. In that moment, I felt it. We were as one. And at the same time, every single one of us was completely separate and unique as well. Just like the sunrise that was breaking through the clouds ahead of us into a gleaming fan of light.

I held the railings as I walked along the deck. A rope was lying unfurled in front of me. Without thinking about it, I picked up the rope and started to wind it around my arm, in a neat loop.

People around me all doing their thing. Working together, each in their own way. The ship was a well-oiled machine. It was perfect.

And among the cogs of the machine, I took my place.

I was heading home, back to the place I knew, to the family that I belonged with. But in the meantime, I was here — and, for now, I didn't want anything else.

I smiled as I worked. I closed my eyes and felt the warmth of the rising sun on my face, the breeze in my hair. And as the day dawned, the ship sailed forward, starting a new journey, forging its own path.

Get your net ready to
catch the first six books,
together in one box!

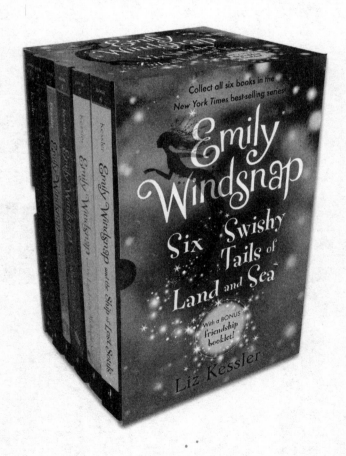

www.candlewick.com

Dive in and read the
New York Times *best-selling series!*

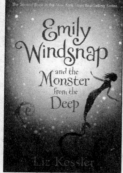

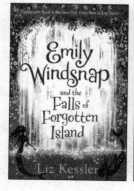

www.candlewick.com

Also from
LIZ KESSLER,
three novels of friendship, family, and magic

What would you do if you knew what the future held?

Available in paperback and as an e-book

A night
of storms.
A lifetime
of secrets.
A week to
find the truth.

*Available in hardcover and
paperback and as an e-book*

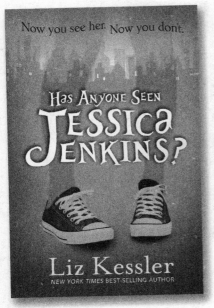

Jessica has a
superpower!
But where did
it come from?

*Available in hardcover and
paperback and as an e-book*

What would you do if you had a fairy godsister?

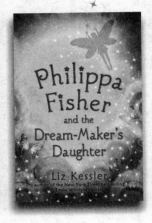

Available in hardcover, paperback, and audio and as e-books

www.candlewick.com